THE MISSING WIFE

DI SALLY PARKER #7

M A COMLEY

ACKNOWLEDGMENTS

Special thanks as always go to @studioenp for their superb cover design expertise.

My heartfelt thanks go to my wonderful editor Emmy, my proofreaders Joseph, Barbara and Jacqueline for spotting all the lingering nits.

Thank you also to my amazing ARC group who help to keep me sane during this process.

Thank you, Jackie Swan for allowing me to use your name as a character.

To Mary, gone, but never forgotten. I hope you found the peace you were searching for my dear friend.

ALSO BY M A COMLEY

Prowlers (Hero #7)

Sole Intention (Intention series #1)

Grave Intention (Intention series #2)

Devious Intention (Intention #3)

Merry Widow (A Lorne Simpkins short story)

It's A Dog's Life (A Lorne Simpkins short story)

Cozy Mystery Series

Murder at the Wedding

Murder at the Hotel

Murder by the Sea

Death on the Coast

Death By Association

A Time To Heal (A Sweet Romance)

A Time For Change (A Sweet Romance)

High Spirits

The Temptation series (Romantic Suspense/New Adult Novellas)

Past Temptation

Lost Temptation

PROLOGUE

 *welve years earlier.*

"So, I told her to forget it. I didn't need that sort of hassle at work," Jackie said.

"Way to go, girl. I wouldn't have allowed her to do it either, bloody cheek. What did she say after that?" Serena took a sip from her wine glass.

Feeling more relaxed than when she'd first arrived at the party, Jackie smiled and ran a finger around the rim of her glass. "She swept her long golden mane over her shoulder and stormed off in a huff. She remained distant for the rest of the week, which was a bonus."

Serena laughed. "And what happened after the week was up?"

"She came crawling back to me and apologised. I couldn't believe it. Mind you, my boss was watching the proceedings, so I'm guessing he had something to do with her unenthusiastic apology."

"Shame on Grant for not sorting it out sooner."

"Yeah, maybe he's the type who gets a kick out of watching catfights between women colleagues. You know, false nails at ten paces, that sort of thing."

Serena laughed. "You're hilarious. It's all hunky-dory again at work now, though, isn't it?"

"Yeah, it's all calm, noses to the grindstone at the moment, what with the summer holidays just around the corner."

"Talking of which, what plans do you have this year?"

"I'm not sure. Robert keeps hinting at going to an island in Greece again, but I'm leaning towards a Caribbean holiday or maybe even the Maldives. I fancy gazing at tranquil blue seas and having baking-hot white sand beneath my feet."

"Umm… the bank balance won't stretch to that expense, I've already told you," Robert hollered, letting her know he was listening in on their conversation.

She wrinkled her nose at him. "See, I never get my way."

Serena laughed. "Hey, you fare better than most women I know. You've had a new kitchen this year and your garden landscaped, which looks stunning, by the way."

"I know. I'm not complaining, believe me. It would just be nice to have a lazy holiday, sunning myself on the beach all the time, without a care in the world. I know if we go to one of the Greek islands, we'll end up exploring it on scooters. Did I mention how scared shitless I am of those things?"

"What's to be scared of, when you've got a hunk like Robert to protect you?"

Jackie glanced over in Robert's direction; he was beaming at the compliment. "Oh no, now look what you've gone and done, he'll probably live off that praise all week, knowing him, reminding me about it at every opportunity."

"Don't you know it," Robert replied.

Serena smirked. "You two are adorable together."

Jackie noticed the glare Serena gave her husband across

2

the other side of the room. He was deep in conversation with one of the other husbands, not giving a damn what was being said, unlike Robert.

"Hey, enough about us, where are you and Denis going this year?"

"You'd be better off asking him that question. I never get a say in any decision-making that takes place in our house."

Jackie lay her hand over Serena's and whispered, "Are things still bad between you two?"

Serena sniffled. "Understatement of the century, love. I seem to piss him off every time I take a flaming breath."

"No, don't say that. Things can't have deteriorated that much, not since I last saw you."

Serena wiped away a tear and lowered her voice further still. "Believe me, it's as bad as it gets. I swear he's having an affair."

Jackie gasped, and her gaze darted towards Denis, who was oblivious to their conversation. "Are you sure? No, he wouldn't dare."

"Trust me, he would. It's not the first time either. Only last month I caught him whispering sweet nothings into that flipping mobile of his. When I challenged him about it, he confessed, assured me he would end it. Bloody liar. Once a cheater always a fucking cheater, that's what Mum used to say, bless her soul. I should've listened to the warning signs during our early days. Mum warned me he had a wandering eye, even back then. I brushed her opinion aside, thought she was being nasty because she always wanted me to marry the wimp next door to us, you remember him, Gary Ponso." She let out a guttural moan. "God, how on earth do I still remember his name, after all these years?"

"It's odd what our memory can recall at times. I didn't know you were unhappy, love. You know I'm always here if you need to vent at any time. A problem shared and all that."

3

Serena sniffed and leaned forward to plant a kiss on her cheek. "You're the bestest of best friends, Jackie. I'd be lost without you by my side, I swear I would."

"I'll always be here for you, you know that, right?"

Serena glanced up and smiled. "I do. You're my one true friend in this world. None of my other friends would willingly sit there and listen to my woes."

"Nonsense. You've got a great sister in Lisa."

"Except she told me at the weekend that she's moving away to London with her new fella. I'm going to miss her terribly, but I can't stand in her way."

"Be happy for her, Serena. She's young, a free spirit. She's braver than either of us and she's got more balls than most men I know."

"Yeah, I suppose you're right, but then, she's only nineteen, so I'm bound to have concerns about her well-being down there. You hear so many scare stories concerning young women, and let's face it, she's only known her boyfriend less than six months."

"Crikey, I didn't realise it was as short as that. What are your parents' thoughts about her decision?"

Serena shrugged. "They're fine with it. Told her the world is her oyster and to be happy. I think Mum, in particular, was a tad envious of her. Not that she would be brave enough to say it out loud. Our family is so messed up."

"Sorry to hear that. My family is the complete opposite, we can be too open with each other at times."

"Hey, I'd rather have your family than mine, at least they care." She waved her hand. "Ignore me, I didn't mean to put a downer on the evening. Smile and be happy, promise me?"

They clinked their glasses together, and Jackie's gaze drifted over to Robert. His eyes had formed tiny slits. He raised his glass to her, and a glimmer of a smile appeared. Jackie chose to ignore him and dragged Serena over to the buffet table. "Come on, we need to dig in or all this food is going to go to waste."

"I can't, I'll never fit into my jeans in the morning."

"So buy a new pair, in a larger size. Look at you, you're far too skinny, Serena."

"I am not, I dispute that. I'm slim with stunning curves in all the right places."

"Okay, if that's how you want to perceive yourself, who am I to argue with you? I'm going to tuck in, it all looks scrumptious, far too good to pass up." Jackie filled her plate high with pastries, chicken wings dipped in different sauces, sausage rolls and mini vol-au-vents, all with spicy fillings. Every item tickled her taste buds and set her senses alight. "Wow, you have to try this." She held out one of the vol-au-vents, but Serena turned her head away.

"A moment on the lips…"

"Who gives a shit?" Jackie murmured. "Life's too short to spend half your life starving yourself just to please a man who treats you like dirt." She cringed as the words propelled out of her mouth at the rate of a torpedo.

"Thanks very much. I told you something in confidence, not expecting you to use it against me." Tears welled up, and Serena wiped her nose with a hanky.

"Damn. I'm sorry. Me and my big mouth. I didn't mean anything by it. It's the drink talking. Ignore me, love."

"I'll leave you to your food, I'm going to the ladies.'" Serena stormed off, catching her shoulder on a few people as she tore through the crowded room.

Robert appeared beside her moments later. "Making a nuisance of yourself again?"

She threw her half-eaten plate of food on the table and faced him. "I beg your pardon?"

"Calm down. You've had too much to drink as usual. Don't make a show of yourself."

5

She stamped her foot. "How dare you say that? How the fuck would you even know that? You've been stuck on the other side of the room for most of the night, no doubt discussing bloody business, as always."

"That's what men tend to do at gatherings such as this, you know that, so why are you so intent on raising the subject every time, causing another senseless argument?"

Heat hit Jackie's cheeks when several sets of eyes landed upon her. "I've had enough. I'm going home."

"I'll get you a taxi then."

She stood her ground and glared at him. "What? You'll take me home, whether you're ready to leave or not."

Robert rolled his eyes and sighed. "Get your coat. I'll make our excuses and take you home if that's what you really want."

"It is." Jackie blustered past him and into the hallway where she shrugged on her coat.

Serena emerged from the downstairs toilet and said, "You're not going home, are you?"

"Yes. Sorry, Serena, I've got a headache."

"What a shame. Are we still up for lunch in town this week?"

"Yes, I'll check my schedule and get back to you in the morning, how's that?"

"Wonderful. I'll look forward to it. Nothing too fancy, though."

"I promise. Or too filling, eh?"

"Don't start, Jackie." Serena left the hallway and went back to the party which was still in full swing.

Robert joined Jackie a few moments later. He held out his arm, she slipped hers through his, and they left the house and walked out to the car. Their home was only a couple of miles away, through the country lanes. Although Robert had drunk a fair amount during the evening, he always managed to get them home in one piece. She felt safe with him, as far as his driving was concerned, at least.

Once they were seated and belted up in the car, he started the engine and drove off. "Why do you always have to cause a scene?"

She swiftly turned to face him, regretting her decision when the wooziness hit her. "I don't and I didn't."

"That's bollocks and you know it. You upset Serena, that's why she made her excuses and went to the toilet."

"Sod off. I told her a few home truths. She keeps herself pencil slim and for what? Her husband is a frigging jerk who pokes every pretty female within ten feet of him."

"Grow up! He does not. What proof do you have of that?"

She folded her arms, annoyed at the condescending way he was speaking to her. "I know he's cheating on her, and she knows it, too. Why women put up with that shit, I'll never know. If I ever found out you were cheating on me, I'd slice it off and feed it to the dogs."

He tipped his head back and laughed. "You're hilarious when you're drunk."

"I am *not* drunk, stop bloody insulting me."

"I wasn't."

Halfway down a country lane, the car juddered for a moment or two and then died on them. "What the fuck is going on?" Jackie demanded.

Robert slammed his palm onto the steering wheel. "Shit, shit, shit. Why didn't I fill up? I should have done it on the way home from work and I got distracted with a business phone call."

"You're kidding me? Call a taxi."

He withdrew his phone from his pocket, stared at it and then faced her with a sheepish expression. "It's dead. I was supposed to charge it when I got home and I forgot."

7

"You're such a useless prick. I intentionally left my phone at home tonight. I suggest you start walking. I'll stay here."

"What? You'd be better off coming with me. I can't leave you out here like this. A car could come around the corner and smash into the back of us any second. It's not safe."

She held up her foot and pointed at the three-inch strappy heels she was wearing. "I am not walking through country lanes in these babies. I'd have dozens of blisters in no time at all. I refuse to do it."

"Whatever. I'm out of here. There's a garage about a mile up the road. I'll check the boot first, see if the petrol canister is in there."

"Good thinking."

Robert searched the boot then popped back and said, "No such luck, I think I took it out to top up the lawnmower a few weeks ago and overlooked putting it back again."

She clapped him. "Brilliant! Well done, you."

"Do me a favour and wind your neck in, Jackie. I'll be back soon."

Jackie stared ahead of her, furious about his incompetence. She watched him walk in the darkness ahead until she could no longer make him out, then she closed her eyes and quickly drifted off to sleep.

A waft of air touched her face. She eased open an eye to find a person, wearing a ski mask, a few inches in front of her. Her first instinct was to scream then she launched herself backwards against the passenger door. Her heart hammered and her skin suddenly went cold. "What? Who are you? My husband will be back any second now."

The masked person ignored her and dug into their pocket to pull out a length of rope and a gun. "Hands. Now."

She had no idea if the gun was a real one or not, there was no way of telling in the dark. "Why? What are you going to do to me?"

8

"Hands."

Jackie shook her head. Suddenly a fist connected with her nose. Bone shattered, and blood erupted along with a burst of sharp pain. A metallic taste filled her mouth. "What did you do that for? Please, don't hit me again."

"Hands."

Three times the person had said the same word, and for the third time, it pissed her off. "No. I won't." This time she was quick to react and dodged a second blow to her face.

But the person punched her in the stomach instead. A second punch and then a jab to her middle followed. Winding her. Reluctantly, she conceded and offered up her hands. Her assailant wrapped the rope around her wrists and then tugged her across the seats, out onto the road, and pushed her towards a vehicle she recognised, sitting behind her husband's car. However, she didn't react.

The assailant led her to the rear of the car and opened the boot.

"No, please. Don't do this to me. What do you want from me?"

"Get in."

"I can't."

Two hands pushed her, sending her off balance. She tipped into the car and stared at him in horror, terrified to move.

Her assailant removed a roll of gaffer tape from a bag close to her head, tore off a strip and placed it over Jackie's mouth. That's when the tears emerged and a sinking feeling of helplessness swamped her. *Why did Robert run out of petrol? All this is his fault. Why did he take off and leave me here? Why didn't he insist that she went with him? Why? Why? Why?*

The boot lid dropped, leaving her fraught with fear. *Oh God, please help me!*

She strained her ear; the car started up and sped away, so

fast she was flung around in the tiny space, bashing her head several times on the objects surrounding her. She reached around, searching for something she could use as a possible weapon, fearing she was going to need one. The car travelled for what seemed like an hour or more and then turned off the main road onto a gravelled area and drew to a halt. The door slammed, and footsteps approached. She prepared to strike with the makeshift weapon she'd found, which felt like a wrench of sorts. The boot opened, and he was standing there, no mask this time. She was right. She'd recognised the car as his.

"Why are you doing this to me? Why?" Her words were pointless, her voice deadened by the tape.

He ignored her. Roughly grasped her hands and lifted her out of the car, whilst she was in a daze. He removed the wrench from her hand without any trouble and threw it back in the car. Then he grabbed a black bag from the boot and pushed her ahead of him, their path guided by the torch he was holding.

"Why? What have I ever done to you? What are you going to do with me?" she tried again. A sob caught in her throat, and tears licked at her cheeks.

Still, he remained silent. He nudged her in the back when her pace slowed. They were deep into a forest now. She glanced before her and spotted a mound of earth ahead of her. Her pace slowed as she realised what this meant.

She turned to face the man and pleaded with him. "Please, no. You can't do this to me. Please, don't do it! What have I ever done to you?"

His response was to nudge her in the back again. Forcing her closer still to her destiny. The mound was in reach now, and her gaze remained drawn to the huge hole that had been dug next to it. Sizeable enough to fit a body, *her* body. She wasn't a religious person by any means, but she found herself turning to God for help. Still her torture continued.

The man yanked on her arm, bringing her to a standstill alongside the hole. The black bag rustled behind her, and suddenly the darkness descended when something rough was placed over her head and covered her body. She tried to scream, but it was futile. She was doomed. Jackie attempted to run, but his large hands clasped her arms.

"I've been waiting for this opportunity to arise." He laughed. Her stomach churned, and she willed herself not to be sick, aware she might choke on her own vomit. *Oh God, is this where my life ends? Please intervene. Don't let this happen to me.*

Whack!

It was the last she heard or felt until she woke up minutes, maybe hours, later. Darkness surrounding her, feeling oppressed by the weight pressing down on her. The scratchy material rubbing against her skin, her face, her hands and her neck. Panic set in as it dawned on her that she was confined to one position, unable to move an inch. *I'm going to suffocate. I don't want to die.*

CHAPTER 1

*S*ally exited the car with a spring in her step. She'd already spotted Lorne's car a few spaces to the left of hers. She rushed over to welcome her. "Hey, you. You lost me back there. I was following you until you put your foot down and left me for dust."

"Oh, was that you following me? I thought it was some lunatic." Lorne smiled.

Sally slapped her upper arm. "Yeah, right. Well, how do you feel this morning? What with this being your first day on the job, *again*."

"Yeah, *again*. I've been in and out of the force so many times over the years, I've lost count now. How do I feel? Hmm... like this is my first day at school. Have I told you how much I hated school, back in the day?"

Sally winked. "I'm surprised you can remember that far back."

"Wow, what a cheek. Is it appropriate to hit my boss on the first day?"

"No, maybe the second. I'm open to bribery, though."

"Oh, right, and what form should that come in?"

"Anything sweet, savoury isn't really my bag. I can burn off the calories in the gym at home later."

"Ooo... get you. Okay, I'm partial to a cream cake now and again, too. And yes, I still weigh the same as I did when I joined the force at nineteen."

"Really? Go you. I'm a few pounds heavier with less years on the force under my belt."

Lorne rolled her eyes and pulled a face. "I don't think I'm doing too badly for an old bird. That's Tony's saying by the way, not mine."

They laughed and headed into the building.

Sally stopped to introduce Lorne to the desk sergeant. "The most important man at the helm is Pat here."

Lorne shook his hand. "It's a pleasure to meet you, Pat."

Pat's cheeks reddened. "I'm in awe of you, ma'am."

"Don't be. I've returned to the force as a Detective Sergeant."

"I'm still in awe of you," Pat replied.

The main door opened, and in breezed DCI Mick Green. "Ah, I see the new recruit has arrived. Welcome aboard, Lorne. I can't stop to chat now, we'll catch up later on today. Must dash, I have a conference call booked for nine o'clock with the Super. Good luck, not that you'll need it. I'm sure DI Parker will prove to be an excellent guide on procedures and what is expected from the Cold Case Unit, in other words, will do her very best to keep you in line."

With that he was gone. Leaving Sally staring after him, open-mouthed. A few seconds later she grumbled, "Bloody cheek. Anyone would think I'm a tyrant. I'm as easy-going as they come, aren't I, Pat?"

Pat busied himself with his paperwork.

Sally slapped her hand on the counter, and he looked up at her. "Aren't I? I said."

"Oh, yes, of course. Sorry, ma'am. Umm… what was the question again?"

Lorne laughed.

"Right, that's it. Maybe I should change the way I work around here. Be the tough taskmaster that invariably comes with the rank I've earned over the years."

Lorne and Pat's faces were a picture, until Sally cracked a smile.

"Hey, I can be a wise-arse, too, when the need arises." She turned on her heel. "Warner, come with me."

Lorne joined her on the stairs, looking dubious. "Everything all right, boss?"

"Of course. I love a good wind-up, like the rest of you. Welcome to the crazy house. You're going to fit in well, I can tell."

"I hope so. I have no intention of letting you down after you bending over backwards to give me this opportunity, Sally. Er… sorry, boss."

Sally leaned in and said, "You can still call me Sal when we're alone, got that?"

"Yes, boss."

They entered the incident room to find the rest of the team already hard at work at their desks.

"Morning, gang. You all know Lorne from the case we helped solve a few years ago. I'd like you to give her a warm welcome to the team. I believe she's going to be a valuable asset around here. More to the point, she'll have a wealth of experience we can exploit, which I'm hoping will make us a far more efficient team."

"Oi, are you saying we've been lacking in the past, boss?" her partner, Jack, was quick to point out.

Sally glanced at Lorne and shook her head. "See what I have to put up with? Don't you feel sorry for me? He's always nitpicking, twisting my damn words."

15

Lorne chuckled but wisely kept quiet.

"Unnecessary comment, just saying, boss," Jack complained.

"Wind your neck in, man, I'm joking. Christ, if you don't know when I'm pulling your leg by now, you never will, Jack Blackman."

He made a face at her, leapt out of his seat and pulled out the chair at the next desk. "Here, Lorne, make yourself at home, next to me."

Lorne smiled and fluttered her eyelashes at him. "Why thank you, kind sir. I don't care what Sally, I mean, DI Parker, says about you, I think you're pretty cool."

The room erupted into applause and laughter at Jack's gobsmacked expression.

He returned to his seat and crossed his arms. "Bloody hell, don't tell me I'm going to have two spirited women keeping me in line now? And I'm not talking about the missus either."

"Right, enough of this frivolity. Let's crack on. Oh, and Jack, Lorne takes one sugar and milk in her coffee."

He jumped out of his seat again and crossed the room to the vending machine.

"See, I have him well trained," Sally whispered in Lorne's ear.

"I can tell. Right, where do you want me to start?"

"I want you to begin on the Pickrel case ASAP. We need to get in touch with his previous employer, Harris Paints, I seem to remember. I didn't get around to questioning the owner of the business when Pickrel was banged up because another case landed on my desk, after we'd wrapped up the investigation and, well, to tell you the truth, it slipped my mind to revisit it. Then I had that chat with you, and by the time I got the ball rolling on getting you back on the force, certain things got pushed aside."

"Understandable. Can you point me in the direction of the file?" Lorne asked. "I'll also need to sort out a new login for the computer system as well."

"Joanna can help with that, can't you?"

Joanna smiled. "It would be my pleasure, boss."

"Right, the file is still on my desk, I believe, in the to-be-actioned pile, you know how it is."

"Don't remind me. I'm so pleased I didn't come back as an inspector, I don't think I'd cope with dealing with all that paperwork again." Lorne glanced over at Jack's desk which was piled high with files.

"Yeah, you guessed it, the paperwork can be quite tedious in Cold Case Unit. Take a look in the spare office along the corridor. You'll see a pile of files yet to be sifted through. We're getting there, but it's a slow job. Falkirk left his mark in a massive way."

"Horrendous to think of all those people sitting in prison who were stitched up by him."

Sally nodded. "We've done our very best to right the wrongs with those already locked up. It's the number of people who died in prison before we could release them that remains a bone of contention with me and weighs heavily on my conscience."

"Why? It wasn't your fault he was sodding bent."

"I know. I guess I'm like you in that respect, we feel guilty even when we're not to blame. Can't help it, can we? I used to colour up at school in assembly if the headmaster gave us a lecture about vandalising the toilets." She laughed.

"Umm... funny you should say that, so did I."

"Proves my point then, doesn't it?"

Jack appeared with a couple of cups of coffee. "Here you are, Lorne, welcome to the team."

"I'll pay you back later, Jack. Thanks."

"No need. Call it a welcome present."

"Much appreciated." Lorne sipped at her coffee and raised her cup. "Spot on, just the way I like it. Wet and bitter. I see the coffee is the same up here as back in London, ghastly."

"Never a truer word spoken." Sally sniggered. "Right, I must get on. I guess I'll buy my own coffee, eh, Jack?"

He puffed out his cheeks and left his desk again. Returning moments later with a steaming cup for Sally. "There you go, boss. Wouldn't want to leave you out now, would I?"

"Ah, but you did. Thanks, Jack. I'll be in my office. Take care of the new recruit for me."

"She'll be safe in my hands, don't worry."

Sally raised her eyebrows. "If you insist. If he gets too enthusiastic and starts mithering you, Lorne, you know where I am. Although, I think you're more than capable of handling him yourself."

"Oi, bloody cheek. I'm a real gent, I am," Jack countered, seemingly offended.

"I'm sure Jack will treat me accordingly." Lorne smirked.

Sally left them to it and entered her office to sift through the usual mass of brown envelopes. She had hoped, starting up the Cold Case Unit would mean she would have less paperwork to deal with from headquarters in particular, but so far, it hadn't turned out that way. She busied herself for the next couple of hours and returned to the team. Sally made a beeline for Lorne who had her head down, looking through some files she'd presumably pulled from the pile in the other room.

"How are you doing?"

"Okay, I think. The team have been really helpful, telling me all about the case, so I'm up to speed on that. I've called the paint company and made arrangements to drop by and see the manager later on; he's busy all morning with reps and holding interviews. I told him I'd visit him at around twelve, if that's okay with you?"

Sally smiled and shrugged. "You don't need my permission to chase up the evidence, Lorne, let's get that straight from the outset. Why don't you team up with Jordan?"

Jordan left his seat to join them. He was smartly dressed, a clean-cut young man any woman would be eager to take home to their mother for approval. He held out his hand for Lorne to shake. "It's going to be an honour working alongside you, Lorne. Your reputation precedes you."

Lorne smiled. "Likewise, Jordan. Thanks for volunteering to spend a lot of time with an old-timer."

They all laughed. Sally felt fortunate, not for the first time, to have a fantastic group of characters surrounding her. Even Jack had got over his reluctance to be a part of the team nowadays. She recalled how childish he'd been, stamping his feet at the beginning, when the team had been initially created.

"Right. Let's get back to it. Have you all picked out a new case to work on?"

Each member of the team either nodded or held up a manilla folder.

"Good. Well, carry on, you know the drill, if anything doesn't sit well with you and you think we should investigate certain aspects further, then give me a shout. Lorne and Jordan, I'll go through the angles you should investigate on the Pickrel case. Shall we take it into my office?"

Lorne and Jordan followed Sally into her office, and they all took a seat. "Right, so, what I gathered from interviewing Louie Pickrel—bearing in mind he might be leading us astray with the information he divulged, there's always that possibility—he reckons there are another nine victims out there, on top of the two little girls we know he murdered."

Lorne shook her head, clearly disgusted. "And you think all his victims were children?"

Sally shrugged. "Who knows? I'm inclined to think yes, but I need you both to keep an open mind, just in case. Question the people Pickrel worked with as well as the boss of the company. See what his relationships were like with his female colleagues. If he had a record for sexual harassment, verbal abuse, that type of thing. Again, we should have covered it the first time around, but once we had him in custody and he admitted to the crimes, I deemed it wasn't necessary to probe further, but then I was hoping that you and Tony would do some digging for me on the side—not in a million years did I ever think you would join the force again, Lorne. We're privileged and honoured to have you as a member of our team. We still have so many cases vying for our attention. With you on board the task is going to be so much easier now."

"Blimey, hey, talk about heaping responsibility on my shoulders. Please also bear in mind I've never had to deal with a cold case before either."

"You'll be fine. Won't she, Jordan?"

"I'd say so. We've all had to adjust to investigating things in a different way than when the victims were still alive. It kind of comes with the territory."

Sally nodded. "Well said. It'll take time for you to get your head around certain aspects of the job, but I have every faith in you accomplishing the mammoth task that lies ahead."

"Umm... you're not really selling it to me, boss." Lorne chuckled. "I'll give the job my all, you know that. If I have any queries, I'm sure Jordan and the rest of the team will be kind enough to lend me a hand."

"Too right we will. We've got your back, Lorne." Jordan grinned.

"Right. So, once you've been to see Pickrel's colleagues, what then?"

Lorne's mouth turned down at the sides. "I suppose it depends on what we find out. Umm... I've been mulling things over, and maybe we should consider visiting Pickrel."

Inclining her head, Sally asked, "May I ask why?"

"I'd like to get to know him a bit more. You never know, he might be willing to talk to us, reveal all, after being banged up for months. Being in a cell twenty-four-seven, or near as damn it, can have a devastating effect on one's mind, so I'm led to believe."

Sally drifted off for a second, pondered if that was true in the case of her ex. "It's got to be worth a try. Just keep me updated on where you are at all times. Apart from that, I'm giving you free rein to go pretty much anywhere and to question anyone you feel you should interview, regarding the investigation. Pretty much anything goes around here. The victims deserve to be identified, and we need justice to be served in their names. The families deserve closure, that's what this team is all about."

"I agree. What about Pickrel's wife? Would it be okay if Jordan and I paid her a visit?"

"I don't see why not. She was heavily pregnant last time I heard, so maybe she's had the child by now. Go easy on her, though, all this came as a shock to her, from what I can remember."

"We'll tread carefully. I'm not saying she'll be privy to anything, but it's an angle I think we should cover all the same. Maybe she's visited him in prison and he's confided in her."

"Or maybe he's cut her off, as some murderers do. Maybe he used her to give himself a persona that everyone would warm to, when all the time he was plotting the deaths of

21

innocent children. Oh gosh, I'm guilty of letting my mind run away with me there. I'll leave it in your capable hands."

"Thanks, boss. We'll be supersensitive, wouldn't want to upset her more than is necessary, she's probably been through the mill since he was arrested and exposed through the court system."

"I think you're right. Okay, anything else you can think of which you need to cover?"

Lorne and Jordan both shook their heads.

"There you have it then, let your onerous task begin. Good luck. I'm always on the end of a phone or here in person if you need any advice."

Lorne and Jordan left Sally to tackle her paperwork in peace. She took time out to check in on her mother, who had been ill over the weekend. "Hi, Mum, I didn't disturb you, did I?"

"Sally, how wonderful to hear from you. No, dear, I'm up and about today, couldn't bear staying in bed another day. Bored out of my mind, I was. I feel sorry for those poor souls who are bedbound in our society, their lives must be totally miserable."

"Glad you're feeling better. Don't go overdoing things now you're up on your feet again."

"I won't. I have a few chutneys to make from the fruit we've gathered from the garden, that shouldn't take me long. Providing I have enough jars to fill, that is. I suppose I'd better check before I start peeling the mound of fruit I have."

"Sounds delicious but hard work all the same. Are you sure you're well enough to get involved in all that today, Mum?"

"Stop fussing. I'm fine, fit as a fiddle and raring to go. You know I rarely sit down around here."

"Yes, that's what's concerning me. How's Dad?"

"He left first thing. He's gone to check on progress at the

new site. The demolition work begins today on that exten-
sion they're planning on rebuilding."

"Ah, yes, Simon mentioned something about that last
night. Glad to see they're both getting on together. I think
Simon envies Dad being on site every day."

"He's got such an important role to fulfil in his working
life, it would be a shame if he gave that up, love."

"I know. I keep enforcing that upon him. He's an excellent
pathologist, the best in the area as you know, but if his heart
belongs elsewhere, who am I to try and keep his feet
grounded? He's his own person. I refuse to be one of those
wives who keep their husbands under their thumbs."

"I agree. You know your father and I have always prided
ourselves on having the same values in life. I wouldn't have
dreamt of trying to quash his ideas over the years. We're
equal partners in our marriage, always have been and always
will be."

"Exactly. I strive to have a marriage like yours, one day."

"You've got it now, Sally. Simon is a wonderful man, a
thousand, no, a million times better than that other waste of
space you married."

Sally shuddered at the bitter edge of her mother's tone.
Or was it because an unwanted image of the detestable Daryl
had just emerged, front and centre in her mind? She tried her
hardest to push the image aside.

"Sorry, Sally, are you still there? I should never have
referred to that mongrel. I can sense what's going through
your mind now. My heart is bleeding for you."

"Don't be silly. I'm over him, I truly am. It's just that in
certain instances his face appears and pulls me back into the
darkest recesses of my mind again. Don't worry, it won't
affect me for the rest of the day, not like it used to. Hey, did I
tell you Lorne is working alongside me now?"

"You did. How's that working out so far?" Her mother

instantly brightened again; she loved Lorne as much as Sally did. They had enjoyed each other's company several times over the last few months.

"She's settled in nicely. About to tackle her first case this morning. I can see the desire burning inside her, it's evident in her eyes."

"Same old Lorne. You know what they say, you can't keep a good woman down."

"Ain't that the truth?"

"Hey, that insightful adage could be levelled at you, too, love. Don't you forget it. You're a thousand times stronger than you were five years ago. And, well, I'm proud to say I have my daughter back." Her mother sniffled. "Oh dear, now you've set me off."

Sally laughed. "You managed to do that all by yourself, Mum. Don't ever worry about me. I have the perfect life now, one I never see changing."

"Oh yes, you do indeed. And that grand house of yours is simply to die for. Simon is the best thing since sliced bread, isn't he?"

"Can you say that about a person?" Sally chuckled.

"Umm… I just did, didn't I? Anyway, I must crack on, I have lots of peeling, chopping and stirring ahead of me. Oh no, wait, how's Dex? We haven't seen him for a few weeks."

"He's as adorable as ever. I didn't want to burden you with dropping him off to see you, what with you being poorly."

"Nonsense. I could nip around and fetch him before I get to work in the kitchen if you like. The company would do us both the world of good."

"You wouldn't mind?"

"Of course not. I've got your key. You don't set the alarm during the day, do you?"

"No. Only at night. Thanks, he'll be overjoyed to see you

show up. I'll pick him up later, on the way home if that's okay?"

"Don't make promises you can't keep. We'll be in touch later. I can always drop him off for you when your father gets home. He'd love to see him as well, he's missed him."

"He's such a wonderful dog. He's fortunate he has three, no, make that four, people who worship him the way we all do. Okay, I'd better get back to work, Mum. Glad you're feeling better. I'll see you later."

"You will. Have a good day, dear."

Sally ended the call and tore open the first brown envelope with her name on it from a pile she'd missed earlier. She was just reading the brain-numbing letter from headquarters when her phone rang. "Hello, DI Sally Parker, how can I help?"

"Hello, DI Parker, I'm not sure if you'll remember me or not. We met a few months ago on the Holly Kilpatrick case. It's DS Jessop here."

Sally raised an eyebrow. She recalled her falling-out with the sergeant about him handing the case over to her as it was related to the Pickrel case, which ended up being the reason they had finally caught up with the suspect. "Of course I remember you. What can I do for you, Sergeant?"

He cleared his throat and sighed. "Umm… I wanted to run something by you if that's all right?"

Sally relaxed into her chair. "Go on, I'm listening."

"I'm working on a case where a skeleton was found buried in the woods. Well, the pathologist has just rung me, you know him, I believe." He snorted, then added, "He's told me that the body was likely buried between ten to fifteen years ago, meaning that it's classed as a cold case now. Would you be interested in taking it on?"

"Yes, definitely. Can you drop the file off to me?"

"Are you telling me your husband hasn't mentioned the case to you?"

"That's right. We have an understanding never to discuss our relevant jobs at home; it has worked out well for us in the past."

"Wow, not sure that would be on the cards for me and my wife. She wants to know the ins and outs of every case I get involved with. She's quite morbid in her outlook, though."

"I hope you don't tell her every single detail of the cases you work on, it's against the force's policy."

"No, only dribs and drabs. She drools, literally, wanting to know more. Hard to keep things from her at times. I get crucified when certain facts come out in the media and I haven't told her."

"Ouch, she sounds a bundle of fun to live with."

He laughed. "Not really. I'll drop the file over now."

"I'll see you soon."

She sat at her desk for another ten minutes, going through her post, until Jack poked his head around her office door. "DS Jessop is here to see you, boss. He told me you're expecting him."

"That's right. Send him through, Jack. I want you to join us as well if you're not too busy."

"Rightio. Sounds intriguing."

Brian Jessop appeared in the doorway moments later. "Hi, it's good to see you again, Brian. Come in and take a seat. All right if my partner joins us?"

He nodded. "Fine by me. I hope you didn't mind me contacting you about this, DI Parker."

"Not at all. Why don't you give me a brief rundown on what you know? After that, I'll contact the pathology department and see what they have to say about the case."

He lowered himself into the chair opposite her, and Jack

sat alongside him. Sally motioned for Jack to look through the file Jessop had placed on the desk.

"The remains were found on Thompson Common. They're felling some dying trees in the area and replanting with new saplings. Anyway, the diggers moved in and unearthed the bones. As soon as the driver spotted them, he called in the necessary authorities and the work was put on hold until the skeleton was removed from the site."

"Okay. You say it was a skeleton, do we know the gender of the corpse?"

"The pathologist said it was likely to be female, judging by the width of the hip bones, but couldn't really give me any more than that. Maybe you'll have better luck on that one. At the time of the burial, the body was wrapped in some kind of hessian; it had deteriorated considerably over the years. We know enough that it appeared to be some kind of sack, and there was enough of it left to make out that it ran the length of the body."

"Any possible cause of death? Sorry, first things first, when were the remains found?"

"Two days ago. It's been a frustrating time for me trying to get the relevant answers from the pathologist. No disrespect, ma'am."

"None taken. In his defence, he's overwhelmed with other cases, him being the only pathologist in the area at present, so we should both give him some slack there. Any current on-going investigations would take precedence over a possible cold case. I know it shouldn't, but needs must, you know that."

"Yep, it's not something that crossed my mind. I was wrong to condemn him."

"No, you weren't, well, okay, yes, you were. We're all under the cosh, with both time and funding restraints in place as usual. I'll have a word with him, go and see him,

27

that'll be the best idea, see what other facts he can tell us. Is that it, as far as you're concerned?"

"I think so. I just thought after the debacle of the last investigation, I would seek out your advice early on this one."

"See, you are a wise man after all. Joking aside, I'm always here if you're ever unsure about a case."

Jessop nodded and rose from his seat. "Thanks, I appreciate that, ma'am. I'll tell my boss that we're officially handing the investigation over to you then, if that's all right?"

"Of course."

"Umm... can you do me a favour and let me know how you get on and if you end up arresting a perp at the end?"

"That goes without saying. You'll be the first to know, er, after the victim's family have been informed, that is."

"Brilliant. Good luck."

He squeezed past Jack and left the room.

Jack slapped the file on the desk and slid it across to her. "Nothing more to add other than what he's already divulged. Where do we start on this one? I take it we're going to commence work on it ASAP, judging by the look on your face."

"You know me so well, or you think you do. Yes, all right, let me give Simon a call, see if he's available to have a chat in person. I'd rather visit the lab and see what we're up against."

"You're just warped," Jack grumbled. "Are you telling me the photos aren't gruesome enough as it is?"

"Idiot. We need to see the skeleton in person. At least, I do. You can wait in the car if it all gets too much for you, you wuss." She pushed back her chair and stood, grinning at her partner. "Time's a-wasting. Let's get over there."

"Weren't you going to give Simon a call first?"

"Oh yes." She sat down again and shooed him out of the room.

"I'm going, don't worry. I'll leave you two lovebirds to it."

"Sourpuss," she called after him. She made her second call of the day to a member of her family. This was unlike her, but this call was out of necessity, not just for the fun of it. "Ah, I've caught you. How busy are you?"

"Hello. I'm busy enough, as usual. What's up?"

"Jack and I need to drop by and see you."

"Any specific reason?"

"We've been handed a cold case that's on your radar."

"Ah, I'm guessing you're referring to the skeleton that was found on the common two days ago."

"That's right. Are you up to receiving visitors now?"

"Yes, come over. I've got a PM booked for this afternoon, just after lunch. I can squeeze you in and set aside what else I had planned, if you're quick. I'm freeish the rest of the morning. I'll put the kettle on."

"Thanks. We'll be about fifteen minutes."

"Look forward to seeing you then. Drive safely."

Sally tutted. "I will, as I usually do. Oh, by the way, Mum's dropping by to pick Dex up. I have to fetch him before I come home tonight. I hope that's okay?"

"Why are you asking me after the deed has already been actioned?" He laughed. "He's your dog, you do what you want with him. I know you'll do the best for him. How's your mum now? I take it she's feeling a lot better if she's going to fetch Dex."

"She seems fine. She's missed him. Okay, enough already. See you soon."

She ended the call, slipped on her coat and entered the incident room once more. "Are you ready, Jack? Or are you going to stand there all day boring Lorne with your old war wound tales? I take it he's told you he got shot four times while he was a serving soldier, Lorne?"

"Yes, he has. I told him about Tony losing his leg to the Taliban in Afghanistan."

Sally chuckled. "Touché. I bet that shut him up. Come on, Jack, we have an appointment to keep with a skeleton at the mortuary."

They raced down the stairs and out to the car.

"That was unkind, back there, you having a pop at me," Jack said.

Sally frowned and turned to her partner. "What? Are you for real? It was a joke. Hey, matey, if you dish it out, I've got news for you, you need to be able to swallow it down if it's retaliated."

He grumbled something indecipherable and got in the car.

Sally sniggered and then composed herself, joining him with a straight face. She could tell he was pissed off because his arms were folded tightly across his broad chest. "Come on, Jack, don't be in a mood with me, life's too short for that sort of crap."

"Yeah, whatever."

She fired up the engine and drove off, aware of how pointless it was trying to talk some sense into him. Halfway through the journey, she tried her hand again at starting a conversation. "How did Donna's birthday go last week? You never really said."

"It went. We had a family meal out with the girls," he replied abruptly.

"And how are things going between Teresa and her new boyfriend?"

"It's not, not really. He's a loudmouth. If he wasn't with my daughter, I'd belt him one. Always making snide comments about coppers."

"Ouch, that must be tough. Can't Teresa say something to him?"

"I get the impression if she did that, he'd bash her one."

Sally quickly faced him and then turned back to watch

the road ahead. "Bugger, really? I'd hate it if I had any kids and they got involved with the wrong person."

"Yeah, tell me something I don't know. Donna has warned me to bite my tongue or risk losing Teresa and not seeing our granddaughter again."

"Shit! So your hands are well and truly tied then."

He released a long sigh. "Yeah, you could say that. It's frustrating as hell for me, having to keep a civil tongue in my head every time we see him."

"I bet. I'm sorry, mate. Always here if you need a chat, you know that, right?"

"Are you, though? Now your best mate is working with us?"

She cringed at the bitterness in his words. "Is that resentment I hear in your voice, partner?"

Another sigh. "No, far from it. Just ignore me. You've wound me up so tightly, I need a little while to get back to normal again."

"I apologise. I didn't mean to poke fun at you."

"What's done is done."

SALLY ARRIVED at the hospital and parked around the back, close to the mortuary. Simon was in his office, up to his neck in paperwork.

He looked up, smiled at them and placed the file he was dealing with on the desk beside him. "Ah, my two favourite coppers. How are you both?"

"In dire need of a coffee," Jack mumbled.

"Of course. Make yourselves comfortable, the kettle has just boiled."

"While you're making the drinks, what can you tell us about the corpse, or should I say the remains?" Sally asked, sitting in the seat closest to the desk while Jack retrieved another chair from the corner of the room.

"Nothing much, not so far. All I can tell you at present is that we're looking at a female victim. No discernible cause of death yet, hard to tell unless she suffered any broken bones as a result of her death, you know, for instance, if she was strangled et cetera. But there's nothing obvious so far."

Sally shrugged. "So where do we go from here then? Can you give us an indication as to how long the woman has been dead?"

"All I can give is a rough estimate of between ten and fifteen years, but take my word for it, that's a very rough idea. I believe we're looking at a murder case, that much is evident, just because of the way her remains were found, wrapped up in a hessian sack, albeit a disintegrating one, and that she was buried in the woods. All the clothing has disintegrated but we did find a few buttons inside the remains of the cloth. We're fortunate that hessian takes a decade or more to rot."

"Heartbreaking that she's lain undiscovered for so long. I fear this is going to be a tough case for us and for her family."

"Yes, I'll be here to give the family as much support as I can. There would be no point, when we finally identify the victim, letting them see the body. I must advise against that. It would be better for them to remember the woman as she was, not how she is now."

Sally took a sip of her drink and then asked, "So what's the next step in trying to identify the remains?"

"I'll need get some advice from a forensic anthropologist, she'll probably suggest carrying out a facial reconstruction. We'll see what she says."

Sally sat forward. "That's always been something that has fascinated me. Don't tell me the process is likely to take months to complete."

"Perhaps. Depends how busy she is. I could call in a favour with Jilly, that's the person on my radar for the task. I've worked with her on several cases in the area in the past, and she's achieved magnificent results. Let me try and call her while you're both here." He spun through his Rolodex cards, favouring the old filing system rather than relying on his computer, and located the woman's number. "Hello, Jilly, it's Simon Bracknall here. How are you...? And your family? Your girls must be growing fast now."

Sally motioned that time was short and for him to get on with it.

"That's great. Down to the nitty-gritty of why I'm ringing you. I was called out to a crime scene, only to discover that the remains had been likely buried between ten and fifteen years ago, therefore, I'm in dire need of your expert opinion and skill... yes, if you wouldn't mind. I have the detective in charge of the case sitting in front of me, she's an impatient bugger at the best of times." He issued Sally a soppy grin and turned his attention back to what Jilly was saying on the other end of the line. "Fantastic, you know where I am. I'll look forward to seeing you later, we'll catch up properly then over a drink."

Sally raised her eyebrow and sensed Jack turn her way.

Simon flushed and put down the phone. "She's a very old friend, one whose skills and advice I have found invaluable over the years. She's also happily married, as am I. Let that be the end of the matter."

Sally shrugged. "Did I say anything?"

Simon stared at her and chortled. "You didn't have to, the barbed look was enough. Anyway, we should be able to get the ball rolling later on today. She's pretty efficient. If she's taking the time out to come over and see me later, then I'm presuming she has a clear patch at the moment. I'll work my magic on her, don't you worry." He added a wink at the end of his statement.

"Okay, if you say so. I guess the next step is for us to view the skeleton, can we?"

"Do we have to?" Jack grumbled. He kept his focus on Simon and took a sip from his cup.

Sally jabbed him in the thigh. "Yes, we *have* to. It's all part of the investigation."

"Finish your drinks and I'll take you through."

They all downed the last of their coffee, then Sally and Jack followed Simon through the long corridor to the changing room, where they pulled on a set of greens each before they continued on to a room at the end. "I didn't bother putting her in the fridge, didn't see any point."

He opened the door and pointed at a steel table, covered in a white sheet. Once they were all in the room, he carefully removed the sheet to reveal the skeleton. Jack heaved beside her.

"Get a grip, man, it's only like something you would have seen in a biology class at school."

"Don't know what school you went to, but something like that definitely wasn't available in any of my classes." He swallowed and turned away.

Sally rolled her eyes at Simon. "I bet you didn't know he was such a coward. See what I have to put up with every day?" Sally chastised herself for picking on her partner again.

Simon laughed. "Shall we get on with it?"

"Sorry, yes. All right if I step closer?"

"Of course. Feel free to inspect every part of her. The team and I have worked day and night to piece her together so quickly."

Sally started at the skull and moved down the table to the feet. She shook her head. "The detail is amazing, not that it can tell us much. Skeletons have always held a certain fascination for me."

"That's because you're warped," Jack groused from his spot close to the door.

She tutted and narrowed her eyes at him. "Whatever." Sally faced her husband and asked, "No possible nicks in the bones?"

"No, I've examined every inch of her in detail, found nothing at all out of the ordinary. I'll get Jilly to give her the once-over when she arrives. I'm sure this will be an absorbing subject for her to sink her teeth into. Her work is amazing. Once she reconstructs the face, you're going to be blown away by the results."

"I hope she's able to do it, for the family's sake. They deserve to know their loved one has been found."

"Yeah, then the hard work for us begins," Jack mumbled from his corner.

"Undoubtedly, but we're up for the challenge, aren't we, partner?"

"If you say so."

Sally glanced up at Simon. "Is there any indication of what she was like at all?"

Simon shook his head. "No, not really. I suppose you're talking about what type of physique she had?"

"Yes. We can tell what her height was, obviously. Can we get her measured up? That will help at our end, when we're trying to match her details to the cases we have on file. Apart from that, I can't think of anything else that is likely to advance such an investigation at this stage."

Simon picked up a tape measure from the table beside him. He handed Sally the metal end to hold and walked the length of the body to the skeleton's feet. "Five feet three inches, below average. The average height of a woman in the UK is around five-four."

"Okay, that's a start," Sally said.

"Great, we know what height she is, bound to make a difference, that is," Jack muttered.

Sally issued a warning glance and shook her head. "Don't push me, Jack. We're doing our best here. Have you got any suggestions? Feel free to chip in when you think of anything useful to add."

He hitched up a shoulder and inhaled a breath, letting it out slowly as he thought. "I suppose you could measure the size of her feet to get her shoe size."

"No need. We have that already, don't forget we found parts of some shoes in the grave with her," Simon replied. "I'll tell you what I could do for you."

"What's that?" Sally asked.

"I could take a photo of the buttons and the shoes found in the grave. Maybe it'll help when you have to meet the relatives."

"Great idea. They're bound to be confused when we tell them. Maybe having the items to hand will help ease the burden on us," Sally confirmed.

"Are we done here?" Simon asked.

"I think so. Yes."

They left the room and disrobed, leaving the green uniforms in the bin in the hallway. "I'll be two minutes. Go back to my office and wait for me."

Jack trudged back up the hallway alongside Sally.

"What is wrong with you?" she demanded, impatiently.

"Nothing. I hate skeletons, and being that close to one makes me physically sick. We can't all be perfect like you. You always take gruesome details in your stride."

"In other words, you're asking me to give you a break?" She smiled at him.

He returned her smile and said sarcastically, "That would be nice, now and again."

Simon joined them a few moments later. He downloaded a couple of photos from his camera, printed them off and then handed them to Sally.

"Thanks, I'm sure this will help. Okay, if there's nothing else, we'll go back to the station and begin trawling through our files. Sorry, what size were the shoes?"

"Six."

"Thanks. I'll see you later." Jack left the room, allowing Sally to give Simon a quick peck on the cheek.

"I'll do my best for you with Jilly. Hopefully we'll get the results back soon for you to make a start on the investigation. I realise what a struggle it's going to be for you without her input."

"Yeah, you could say that. These things are sent to try us, though, I suppose."

Sally caught up with her partner near the main door. It had been raining since they left the car. "I'm going to make a dash for it."

"I was hoping we could stay in the dry a bit longer, it's pissing down out there."

Sally shook her head and bolted out to the car with Jack close behind her. She pressed the key fob, and they slid into their seats. She glanced in the mirror and brushed back the wet hair that was plastered to her face. "Roll on the spring."

"Roll on our trip to Spain in a few weeks, I can't wait."

"I'm envious of you, especially on days like today."

They drove back to the station and bumped into Lorne and Jordan in the car park.

"Hey, where are you two off to?" Sally called across the top of several cars, thankful that the rain had finally stopped.

Lorne smiled and shouted back, "Off to Harris Paints. Is that all right with you?"

Sally smiled. "Of course it is. Let me know how you get on when you get back. Good luck."

"Hopefully we won't be long. Want us to pick up some lunch on the way back? I'm not sure how things work around here, sorry if I'm overstepping the mark with my suggestion."

"Lorne, stop that. We tend to eat when we can. Good idea. We'll all reimburse you when you get back. Want me to text you with everyone's requirements?"

"That'd be great. This one is on me, though."

Sally wagged her finger. "There's no need for that."

"I want to. I'm so thrilled to be part of the team, it's my thank you gift to you all for accepting me."

"Okay, if you insist. But don't make a habit of it, you're not on an inspector's salary now, in case you hadn't noticed."

Lorne laughed. "Yeah, that might have slipped my mind when I made the offer. We shouldn't be long."

"Take your time."

CHAPTER 2

*E*n route, Lorne decided to get the lowdown on her partner. "You obviously know everything there is to know about me, why don't you tell me a bit about yourself, Jordan?"

"I have to say I keep pinching myself, can't believe I'm partnered up with someone of your calibre. You'll have to forgive me if I take a step back and watch you in action at times."

Lorne laughed. "Oh God, please don't treat me any different than you would your other colleagues. I'm nothing special, I can assure you. Hey, this side of things is going to be very diverse for me. I'll be counting on you to put me on the right track most of the time, don't forget that. You're the expert in this field, not me."

"Hardly an expert. The Cold Case Unit has only been up and running a few years. I think we're all still finding our feet. It's a lot tougher than most people realise, you know, what with the crimes taking place years ago. Evidence and clues can be frustrating to come by, I can tell you."

"I can imagine. Let me in, give me a glimpse of your personality."

"Well, I'll be thirty-seven in a couple of weeks. Damn, where has the time gone?"

"Yeah, don't go there, I tend to think that daily at my age. Are you married? Any kids?"

"I've just got engaged to a feisty German artist."

Lorne laughed. "Feisty, eh? What's her name? Does she live in England?"

"Oh, yes. We've been together for the past three years. Ingrid already lived here in the UK. She couldn't wait to leave Germany and moved over here in her teens."

"And what type of artist is she?"

"She paints landscapes for a living. Beautiful they are, she sells them at a local art gallery. I've told her she can do better than that, they're so good." He scrolled through his phone and held up a photo for Lorne to see. Luckily, the lights had changed to red up ahead. She glided to a halt, glanced at the photo and gasped. "Wow, that's absolutely stunning. She's super talented, Jordan."

"Yeah, I keep telling her that, but there are days when she doubts herself."

"I hear that all the time about talented people. They're very insecure, all you can do is be there, to support her. Looking at the sample you've just shown me, I'd say she has nothing to be worried about."

"I've told her that constantly, since the first day I met her. Seriously, I'm in awe of her talent and give her all the support I can muster, however, sometimes, she throws it back in my face."

"That's tough to deal with, I'm sorry. I'm sure it's unintentional. Hang in there. Have you tried to discuss how you feel with her, or do you believe that will only make matters worse?"

He nodded. "The latter, unfortunately. Thanks for listening. The last thing I expected to do today was come to work and offload all my troubles on my new partner."

"Hey, it's what partners are for. I do it all the time. I think men tend to steer away from unburdening themselves, which is daft. It can be therapeutic, as well as enlightening."

"You mean, like getting things from another person's perspective, rather than dwell on my own?"

"Exactly. Feel free to chat anytime you like. I have a wealth of experience on different subjects under my belt."

"Do you want to give me a list?" He laughed.

"It's far too long, just give me a shout when the need arises to ask for a second opinion in the future, okay?" She briefly turned to look at him and smiled.

"I think I'm going to enjoy having the famous Lorne Simpkins/Warner as a partner."

"The feeling is mutual, Jordan. I sense we're going to make a phenomenal team."

"Let's hope so."

They chit-chatted the rest of the way, nothing in depth, like the first topic they'd covered, just general chat about the workings of the team and how every member had needed to develop a different mindset to be able to deal with the cold cases.

"Something I need to get my head around, for sure," Lorne replied. A slight doubt crept into her mind whether she had done the right thing or not. She pushed it away as soon as it reared its head. *Not going there. I'm going to do my very best to ensure I don't regret my decision. There are families out there who will be relying on us to get results.*

"It's the next turning on the left, and if my memory serves me right, it should be at the end of the estate," Jordan said.

"Glad you're here. I would have been going round and

round in circles otherwise. See, that's an impressive foundation for great teamwork already."

Jordan beamed with satisfaction. Lorne drew into the car park in front of the commercial unit, and they both got out of the car.

"Do you want to take the lead?" he asked tentatively.

"I don't mind. I suppose I've been used to being the lead investigator over the years, so it makes no odds to me. As long as we get what we need, right?"

"I agree. Anyway, it'll be good for me to see you in action, so to speak. I'm always eager to learn from those with more experience."

"Then lead I shall, on one proviso."

"What's that?"

She smiled. "You feel free to jump in at any time if you sense me drying up. I'm bound to be a little rusty. After all, it's been a couple of years since I was in the field."

"I've got your back, don't worry."

"Good to know. Let's get in there and see what we can find out. I hope he's not one of these bosses who believe this kind of information is too precious to share."

"We'll soon find out."

Jordan opened the door to the unit and stood back to allow Lorne to enter first. It was a telling sign for her, that one, he was a gentleman, there weren't many of those around these days, and two, he had an unspoken respect for her already.

"Thanks, you're a gent."

The black-haired receptionist with vivid makeup smiled at them as they entered the small reception area. "Hello. How can I help you today?"

Lorne and Jordan flashed their warrant cards.

"We'd like to see Mr Harris, if he's available?" Lorne said.

The woman glanced down at the phone system in front

of her. "He's still on the phone to one of our suppliers. He shouldn't be too long. No, wait, he's completed his call now. I'll nip in there before he starts another conversation. This is a busy time of the month for us." She wheeled her chair back and trotted over to the door behind her and knocked on it.

"Yes, come in, Cheryl."

"Mr Harris, sorry to interrupt. I have a couple of police officers here to see you."

Lorne couldn't hear the man's reply. Instead, the receptionist took a step back, and a balding man in his fifties poked his head around the door to look at them.

"Hello, sir. We just have a few questions to ask, if you can spare us ten minutes or so. If not, we can call back later."

Mr Harris frowned, straightened up and walked towards them. "Questions? Regarding what, may I ask?"

"It would be better if we spoke privately, in your office, Mr Harris," Lorne said. She smiled, trying to cut through the man's uncertainty.

"Very well. Come through. Do you want a drink? Tea or coffee?"

"No, we've not long had one, but thanks for the offer."

She and Jordan skirted around the reception desk and followed Harris into the room. He thanked Cheryl, dismissing her, and closed the door.

After taking his seat, he linked his hands in front of him. "Now, perhaps you'll tell me what all this is about? As far as I know, we haven't been up to anything illegal, so you'll have to forgive me for being perplexed by your visit."

"To put your mind at ease, we're not here regarding the business, not as such. We're from the Cold Case Unit."

His eyes widened, and he sat back, as if a huge weight had been lifted. "A Cold Case Unit? Okay, I'm sorry, I'm afraid I'm none the wiser." He sat forward again and shook his head. "I think the penny has just dropped. Is this about that bastard Pickrel?"

Lorne nodded. "It is. You're obviously aware of what went on in his past."

"Disgraceful. Killing his own sister like that. No, wait, he also killed another little girl, didn't he? Wasn't that how you caught the bastard?"

"It was. During the interview stage with our boss, he revealed that he had killed several others as well. That's why we're here, we're on a mission to try to find where he buried his other victims. That's where you come in, we need your help."

"What? I don't bloody know. Are you suggesting that he confided in me?"

Lorne raised a hand. "Not in the slightest. I'm so sorry if it came across that way. No, what we'd like to obtain is his schedule while he worked for you, is that possible?"

He raised an eyebrow. "You're aware that disgrace of a human being worked for this company for thirteen years, aren't you?"

"We are, sir. I suppose we're here hoping that your records would still be available for us to investigate."

"I see. But thirteen years. In that time, I never had an inkling I was in the presence of a disgusting killer."

"Sometimes it's very hard to tell. It's not like they wear a badge declaring their role in society."

"If he had, do you truly think he would have lasted five minutes around here? He always struck me as a quiet individual. Over the years, not once did I see him lose his temper. Just goes to show you don't really know a person and what's going on inside their head, at all."

"That's true. Can you help us out with the information, Mr Harris?" Lorne prompted again.

"It's Norman. I don't know, maybe Cheryl will be able to cobble together what you need in her spare time. At the moment, I'm up to my neck in work, hectic time of the month, dealing with suppliers both here and abroad. Our jobs have become that much harder now Brexit has occurred, especially regarding all the paperwork we need to fill in to export these days. Something I need to assess, when I have the time."

"Whatever you or Cheryl can give us today would help. All we need is his schedule to know which routes he likely took and when. If we can match his itinerary to any cold cases on file then we can dig further, to see how many more charges we can pin on him."

"God, in that case, yes, I'm sure we will do all we can to help. I hope he rots in Hell for what he's done. To think there are possibly more victims out there, well, it makes my blood run cold. Let me have a word with Cheryl, see if she can get some form of printout for you."

"You're very kind. Thank you, sir."

He left his seat. "Don't go thanking me just yet, I might be left with egg on my face if Cheryl thinks it's a no-go. I won't be long."

Once the door closed behind him, Lorne faced Jordan. "Sounds kind of hopeful."

"Cheryl should be able to come up with the goods, if they're still using the same computer system."

"Hmm... how likely is that, if Pickrel started here over thirteen years ago?"

"Depends on how efficient it is and the needs of the business, I suppose," Jordan pointed out.

Lorne sighed. "I guess we're going to find out soon enough. Let's keep our fingers crossed in the meantime."

Within seconds the door opened, and Mr Harris rejoined them. He took his seat before he spoke. "You're in luck.

Cheryl is on the case now. She reckons she'll have the information for you within twenty minutes."

Lorne blew out a relieved sigh. "Crikey, that's excellent news. We were just debating whether you had the same system you had in place when Pickrel started working here, I suppose you've given us the answer."

He pointed. "Actually, you're in luck. I've been looking into upgrading the system in the summer. I'm in the process of weighing up the costs. These computer companies are keen on charging exorbitant fees, but then, how else are we likely to make the transition? It's a risk I need to look into further, in all honesty. Everything has a cost, a major one at that, attached to it these days. Saying that, we have backup manual paperwork, I wish we could go back to that, you know, dealing with files every day. It would be a darn sight cheaper to employ an extra person to keep it in order for the next ten years, rather than make the switch, I can assure you."

"I'm sure. Why don't we wait outside and leave you to get on with your work?"

"Would you? That would be wonderful. If you're sure I can't be of any further assistance to you."

"Maybe a few more questions then, if that would be all right?"

"Shoot. I'm all yours. What do you need to know?"

"I suppose what I'm after is a possible insight into his character. If he ever showed up for work not acting like himself on the odd occasion, what excuses he gave?"

"No, there were never any trigger signs, not for me. As a salesman, he tended to be on the road most of the time. All his orders came in via the computer. I suppose I saw him a couple of times a month. Or, on the rare occasion when there was a problem with an order. In that respect, he was like a stranger to me and Cheryl. She's sure to back me up on that if you ask her. All this came as a total shock to both of us. We discussed it, you know, around the time the news broke, and neither of us could think of an instance when we had any doubts about his character at all. It bugged me that we didn't know him at all, let alone how dangerous he was. We thank our lucky stars every day that neither of us fell out with him. Lord knows what would have likely happened, given what he's been put away for. Shocking, it is."

"So true. What about other members of staff, did they ever have any grievances with Louie?"

"No, we only ever employed one salesman, a few people at the factory, he never really came into contact with them face to face as all the orders were dealt with via the computer. Then there's Cheryl and myself, of course. She has never raised any issues with me about his conduct towards her over the years. Weren't his victims all children, or am I wrong?"

"Yes, you're correct, although we're going to be keeping an open mind regarding the ages of other possible victims, what with him being on the road a lot. Maybe the urge to kill presented itself in other ways."

He frowned. "I'm not with you?"

"Possibly young hitchhikers, male and female. This is what we're trying to figure out. You're aware of the statistics for missing persons over the years, I take it?"

"Not really, although I can imagine the figure has grown substantially since I was a lad, with youngsters' tolerance levels at an all-time low, according to the number of teenagers being stabbed increasing year on year."

Lorne nodded. "Yes, there's that angle to consider as well. We've definitely got a major task on our hands."

"I can believe it. I don't envy you in the slightest. If we can help in some small way, then it'll be our pleasure to try and ease your burden."

47

"Thank you. We're doing it for the families of the victims. No mean feat, I can tell you."

"I can imagine. Shocking state of affairs. I'm still in disbelief about his arrest and sentencing to be honest with you. He was married, too. What his wife must be thinking about all of this is beyond me."

"Yes, to Natalie. We believe she's recently given birth to his child, too. I can't imagine how she must be dealing with such a travesty. We'll call in and see if there's anything we can do to help."

"That's kind of you. I would ring her to offer my assistance, but, being a man, I wouldn't know where to bloody begin. I'd ask my wife to step in for me, except I got divorced last year." He shook his head, and a sadness cast a shadow over his features. "Thirty years married, and out of the blue, she announces she's had enough and wants a divorce."

"Sorry to hear that. Are you telling me there were no signs that your wife was unhappy?"

He blew out a breath. "Thinking back, the signs were there, but I was too wrapped up in this place to take much notice. And yes, I'm guilty of being a workaholic. I'll slow down eventually, I suppose. I'm knocking on the retirement door with one hand and stepping back from it at the same time, if that makes sense?"

"It does. You'll know when the time is right. In fact, I've recently come out of retirement myself."

He raised an eyebrow and inclined his head. "May I ask why? Did you get bored?"

Lorne chuckled. "Far from it. My husband and I run a dog rescue centre, which is a full-on job in itself. I suppose I missed solving crimes and helping the general public get the justice they deserve. The Cold Case Unit is unknown territory for me. I don't have a clue where it's going to lead or if

48

I'm going to enjoy it as much as 'normal policing', but I'm going to give it my best shot."

"Are you saying you believe that police work is a calling for you?"

She smiled and nodded. "I think you're right. Anyway, enough about me. If there's nothing else you can tell us about Louie, then we'll leave you to it and wait outside."

"I can't for the life of me think of anything. Do you want to leave a card just in case something pops into my head?"

Lorne turned to Jordan. "I haven't got any printed yet, do you have any on you?"

He removed one from his pocket and slid it across the desk. "There you go, sir. We're partners, so if you contact me, I'll pass your message along to DS Warner."

"Good, good. I hope you have a successful investigation. He deserves to spend the rest of his life behind bars for what he's done, none of this half-sentence malarkey, which is a farce. He took two lives, more possibly, he shouldn't be allowed to walk the streets a free man ever again."

"I wholeheartedly agree with you, and we're going to do our very best to ensure that doesn't happen. We can't thank you enough for helping us in this manner, Norman."

He rose and showed them to the door. "You're welcome. I'll leave you in Cheryl's capable hands." Lorne and Jordan shook his outstretched hand. "Do your best."

"We will," Lorne replied with a smile.

When they returned to the reception area, Cheryl instructed them to take a seat. "I'll be another ten minutes at least. Sorry for the delay, the internet is always a bit slow at this time of the day for some reason."

"No problem. It's not like we have to be elsewhere."

Cheryl tapped at a few keys, and the printer churned into life behind her. "That's the first of the reports coming through now."

"Fantastic news. Thanks, Cheryl, this is going to make a vast difference to our investigation."

"It's appalling what he did. I'm only too happy to help if it means putting him away for longer. Disgusting excuse for a human being, although you wouldn't think that by looking at him. Words failed me when Norman, sorry, Mr Harris divulged what he was guilty of. How the heck can that man live with himself? Putting his mother through that for all those years?"

"Murderers don't tend to have consciences. Their main focus is to cause as much harm as they can to a family, especially if they are killers like Pickrel, whose crimes turn out to be premeditated."

"I know he's behind bars now, but do you think he'll ever get out? You hear on the news about all these vile people only serving half their original sentences, why? I can never understand that. It's not right, surely."

"It's the way the system is set up to work. I assure you, you won't find a serving officer who doesn't scratch their heads at some of the bizarre sentences handed down to certain criminals."

"It must be frustrating for you guys. I can see that."

Lorne tutted and shrugged. "It goes with the territory. All we can strive to do is our very best in the hope that the barristers and judge in turn do their utmost further down the line."

"But it doesn't always work out that way, does it?"

"No, far from it. Which is why it's important for us to always dot the i's and cross all the t's."

"Understandable. However, I still wouldn't like your job. I bet it can be thankless at times."

"Yes, but also rewarding at others. We get used to it and endeavour to change things for the best."

Cheryl nodded and walked over to the printer. "That's the

final one now. It should all be in order. I'll slip them into a file for you, protect them from getting wet."

"That'll be much appreciated. Thank you, Cheryl. I'm going to leave you with one of my partner's cards. If you think of anything we should know, will you give him a ring?"

"Of course." Cheryl tucked the papers into a manilla folder and slid it across the desk to Lorne. "I'll try and cast my mind back over the years, see what I can come up with regarding that devil of a man. Lately, I've tried to block his image from my mind. I now know how important any clues might be for you to work with. I'm going to do my best for you in the hope you find the evidence you need to add to his sentence."

"Thank you, we can't ask for more than that. Goodbye, and thanks again for sharing this information with us, I predict we have a long day ahead of us."

"Good luck."

On the way back to the car, Jordan said, "You have such a way with people. Just saying."

Lorne frowned and looked over the top of the car at him. "I do? How do you speak to people then?"

"I've never really thought about it before, however, watching you at work, you put everyone at ease when you speak with them. Not sure if I've managed to master that over the years."

They slipped into their seats and buckled up.

"You'll get there," Lorne said. "I wasn't always as good at communicating with people, I promise you. Actually, I'm surprised I've managed to slip back into the role so quickly."

"I suppose the first question is always the hardest, and everything after that is a doddle."

Lorne laughed. "If you say so." Her mobile pinged, indicating she had a text. "I bet I can guess what this is." She put in her password and saw the text was from Sally. "As I suspected, it's a list of sandwich requirements. We'll pick them up on the way back."

AFTER LUNCH WAS OVER, Sally requested to see Lorne in her office, along with Jordan. "So, how did you get on?"

Lorne settled into her chair and went over what they'd found out at the paint company. "We've come away with his schedule, going back thirteen years. Jordan and I will be busy the rest of the day and probably well into tomorrow, planning out the routes he took every week."

Sally nodded. "Excellent. Although I sense you're going to be up to your eyes in it. Wouldn't he have regular punters? Take the same routes a lot of the time?"

Lorne held her fingers up. "That's what we're hoping. We'll suss his routes out first and then try to match it up to any of the unsolved cases we have to hand. We've got missing person cases as well as unsolved murders, I take it?"

"Not really, there might be some in there, but you'll probably be better off speaking to Misper from the outset, to save a bit of time."

"Good thinking. I'll get on the blower right away. Sorry, I'll get on the phone right away." Lorne chuckled when she saw Sally frown.

"You do that. Good luck."

"How did you get on, boss? At the mortuary?" Jordan asked as Lorne started to leave her seat.

Sally released a sigh. "Our hands are tied for the foreseeable future, at least until the forensic anthropologist has carried out a facial reconstruction. She's calling in to see Simon this afternoon. Hopefully, she'll mark it as urgent."

Lorne nodded. "They can do wonders. I've had to use them a few times over the years and I've been in awe at what they can achieve. The result should give you the impetus to plough on."

Sally smiled. "Here's hoping. Let's get to it, guys."

Lorne and Jordan left the room and got down to planning out the routes right away. After half an hour, Lorne clicked her fingers and cursed under her breath. "I forgot to ring Misper. Can I leave you with this for a second or two?"

"Go for it," Jordan replied.

She went back to her desk to place the call.

"Missing Persons, Miranda speaking. How may I help?"

"Hi, Miranda. I'm DS Lorne Warner with the Cold Case Unit. I was wondering if you could do me a favour."

"I won't know until you tell me what that favour is. I'm all ears. I'll help if I can."

"Good. Sorry, it's my first day back as a detective, you'll have to forgive me if I sound a little rusty."

"You don't, not so far. Have you been on maternity leave?"

Lorne sniggered. "Hardly, I'm a little over the hill for that malarkey. I retired a few years ago and have returned to the force."

"Wow! Are you serious? Blimey, once I retire, there'll be no way back for me. I have too many plans to take care of."

"Each to their own, I suppose. I missed the stress."

They both laughed. "I hope it pays off for you. Now, what can I do to help?"

"I'm asking a lot of you, I know. But I was wondering if you could pull some files for me."

"Go on. Any specific dates?"

"From 2007 to 2020." Lorne cringed, expecting a backlash.

"Really? Thirteen years? What should I be looking for, anything in particular?"

"Let me give you a bit of background and we'll go from there. We've got a man currently serving time for killing his sister. He was a teenager at the time, got away with the crime for years until the urge struck again and he killed another little girl last year. Whilst he was being interviewed, he bragged that he had killed nine more times."

"Jesus, there are definitely some dangerous characters around. So I take it you'll be wanting me to search for young girls?"

"That's just it, I don't know. Logic is telling me that should be the case, but my gut is telling me otherwise. Would it be a problem for you to give us all you have, I mean, to include children and adults, who went missing during that time in the Norfolk area?"

Miranda sucked in a breath. "Goodness, I'll be at it all day. But if that's what you need, then I'm here to help."

"Gosh, you don't know what a relief that is to hear you say that. Thank you so much. When can we expect the report?"

"Give me a couple of hours. I'll get back to you soon. Maybe you could drop by and pick up the results?"

What happened to all day? "Without a doubt. Just give me a ring when you're ready. I can't thank you enough. I realise this is going to be a tough task for you."

"You have no idea. Right, go, let me get on with it. I'll be in touch soon."

"I'll be here, waiting. Thanks, Miranda."

Lorne punched the air and returned to her seat next to Jordan. "That's all sorted. Miranda at Misper reckons there will be a flood of names coming our way. I've given her a range across the board, just in case his MO has altered over the years. Let's face it, we don't know, and he hasn't really hinted at what we should be searching for, has he?"

"Not as far as I know. I'm almost there, planning out the routes. I've highlighted the same route he's taken in red. There really aren't too many roads he could have used, this being Norfolk and so far behind with our road structures, if you get my drift?"

"I do. No motorways to contend with, which might be a good or bad thing, we've yet to determine that. Want a coffee?"

He smiled. "I'll get them, you bought lunch." He left his seat before she could object.

Lorne was getting on well with Jordan, he was smart and charming all rolled into one. *Stop it! I'm a happily married woman, and he's just got himself engaged.* She was still smiling at what was going on in her head when he returned.

"Something amusing you?"

He handed her a plastic cup which burnt her fingertips. She popped it down on the desk and picked up a few of the reports Cheryl had printed off for them. "No, nothing, I promise." Her cheeks reddened under his piercing gaze. She focused on the sheets in her hand which had been high-lighted by her partner. "Why don't we make a start on what we have? We'll need to go through all the files next door. How familiar are you with them?"

"Quite familiar. We've been dipping in and out of them for a few years now. Some of them will be in the dismissed pile. They're the ones we're not going to bother reviewing any more as the convicted criminal has either served his time or passed away."

"Okay, that makes sense to me. I'm sure there will be plenty more left for us to go through."

"Definitely. Shall we take our cups through to the other room, or do you want to take a breather for a few minutes, give our eyes a break?"

She grinned. "I'd rather crack on if it's all the same to you."

They carried their cups into the room along the hallway. Jordan unlocked the door and switched on the light.

"Bloody hell. I didn't realise there were this many files to go through and just how big some of them are."

"I know. People outside of this team don't realise what we're dealing with. Like I said, that pile in the corner, can and should, be ignored. We've gone through the files countless times and come to the same conclusion each time."

"I'll take your word on it. I think we've got enough on our plates as it is. Where do we bloody start? That's the question!"

"Why don't we start on the right and work our way through? I think I should put some heating on first, it's very chilly in here." He marched across the room to the antiquated radiator on the far wall and fiddled with the thermostat. The water immediately circulated the radiator.

Lorne rubbed her hands together to ward off the chill and collected two chairs from the stack in the corner. She placed them in front of the files and sat. Bending forward, she chose the first file and flicked through it.

It took them a few hours of bottom-numbing work to get through the first twenty files. They managed to pull two possible victims from them. "This is going to take us an eternity at this rate, and we have the Misper files to go through yet, no doubt there are going to be a mountain of those as well," Lorne complained. She wriggled in her seat, doing her best to find a more comfortable position. In the end, she got down on the floor.

Jordan laughed.

"What? I used to get on the floor all the time at home. Although nowadays, I think you might need to lend me a hand to get up when I decide to make a move."

"I will. I was just thinking, 'Make yourself at home, Lorne.'"

"Thanks. I will. Now, where were we? Ah yes, going

through this lot. Have you ever started a job and regretted it a few hours later?"

"Frequently, it comes with the territory around here."

I

t was almost five before Lorne received the call from Miranda. "Can you drop by soon? I have to shoot off at about five-fifteen, I need to pick up my cat from the vet's."

"I'm on my way. Nothing serious, I hope?"

"No more kitties for her, she's been fixed, filthy mare. She's had two litters already. Got pregnant with the second litter before we could get her booked in for the op."

"Oh dear. I knew there was a reason I preferred dogs."

"It's not too late for me to change. See you soon."

Lorne ended the call and tried to get up off the floor. "Jesus, why in God's name did I get down here in the first place? Sorry, Jordan, you're going to have to give me a hand."

Jordan laughed and swept into action. He held out both hands and hoisted her to her feet. Embarrassed, she brushed down her trousers and jacket.

"Thank you. I'll reconsider putting us both in that position in the future. I'm going to run up to Misper now. Er... on second thoughts, maybe *run* was the wrong verb to use."

Jordan shook his head and grinned. "Oh God, you crack me up."

"Always good to have a laugh, it brightens the dullest of days, in my experience. My old partner and I..." Unexpected tears welled up as she thought of Pete Childs. She waved a hand and cleared the lump that had appeared in her throat with a cough. "Never mind. We shouldn't dwell on the past."

"Are you referring to the partner who was killed in the line of duty?"

"Yes. I shouldn't have mentioned him, it always gets the waterworks going when I recall the pleasure I had working with him. Damn, if ever he heard me talking like that, he'd laugh his bloody socks off. I used to be a right bitch towards him, he was a lazy so-and-so, but we made a good team. I got the best out of him where other DIs had failed, yes, let's put it that way."

"Such a shame when you have a connection like that with a partner. I hope you don't have regrets working with me in the future."

Lorne rubbed his arm. "I'm sure we're going to make a great team. Now, I must fly. Yes, that's a good verb, if only I could grow a pair of wings." She left Jordan going through yet another file and walked up two flights of stairs to the Misper Department. Out of breath, she pushed open the door and placed her hands on her knees for a second or two while she recovered, until someone came to see her.

"Hi, can I help? Are you Lorne Warner?"

"How could you tell? Don't tell me, it's the fact I'm totally unfit that's given me away, right? Jesus, I need to start going to the gym more if I'm going to be running up and down all the stairs around here daily. I never knew there were so many, and no lift in sight either."

"Ah, no one has bothered to tell you about the lift at the rear of the building, I take it?"

"No. Definitely not. You really think I would have chosen not to use it, had I known about it? Anyway, you must be Miranda, yes?"

"That's right. Come through. I have what you need in the office. Umm... I might need to give you a hand lugging it all back down the stairs."

If Lorne felt tired before, Miranda's comment left her feeling utterly exhausted. "We'll see, show me the way."

She followed Miranda through a couple of screened-off offices, to the one at the rear. There, sitting on her desk, was a pile of paperwork about a foot high. "Geesh! You weren't kidding either."

"I think I have a box here somewhere. We could carry it down the stairs together."

"I'm fine. I'll jump on that lift you mentioned. You need to get off anyway. The box would really help, though, if you can put your hands on it."

Miranda tore next door and returned with an archive box. She scribbled through the label on the front and placed the pile of paperwork inside. She tested it to see if it was too heavy for Lorne to carry. "I think you'll be okay. I'll take it to the lift for you."

"Honestly, you've done enough for me already. I can manage from here."

"Okay, if you insist. Let me fetch my coat and say farewell to the team and I'll show you where the lift is. I might even use it myself for a change. I've been running around here like a blue-arsed fly for most of the day, so there's no need for me to use the stairs on the way out."

Lorne smiled and picked up the box. It wasn't too heavy, but she had a feeling it would get heavier over time. Miranda grabbed her coat and bag and shouted goodbye to the rest of her colleagues on the way out. She opened the door for Lorne, and together they jumped into the lift. Miranda pressed the button for Lorne's floor, and the old lift juddered into action, squealing its objection at being used.

"Crikey, I take it this isn't used much during the day?"

"No, rarely, in fact."

"I think this will be my first and last time, unless I'm desperate." The doors opened on Lorne's floor. She picked up the box and walked out. "Hope your pussy is all right when you get home. Thanks for all your help today, Miranda."

"All part of the service. I hope it helps. Let me know how you get on, if you would?"

"I'll be sure to do that. Have a good evening." Lorne smiled and turned to lug the box the rest of the way back to the room where she'd left her partner. She kicked the door open.

Jordan leapt out of his seat and ran a hand through his dark-brown hair. "Jesus, you scared the shit out of me."

Lorne bit her lip and crushed a smile. "Sorry about that. This thing is heavy."

He rushed forward and took the box from her and placed it on a nearby desk. "You should have called me, I would have come and collected it for you."

"Hey, it's okay. Good to know for the future, though. Looking at this lot, we've got our work cut out for us. How have you got on in my absence?"

"I put another case file on the *possible* pile."

"It seems that going through this lot is going to take us a fair few days, is that the usual crack around here?"

"It can be, unless some important information drops into our laps from the word go. It's a major downside to working cold cases, nothing is current. If anything, we're left scratching our heads even more than when working on 'regular crimes'."

"I think I'm beginning to understand that already. Want another drink before we start on this lot?"

"I'll get it, if you like?"

With that, Sally appeared in the doorway. "How's it going in here?" She reviewed the contents of the floor and shook her head. "Not so good by the look of things."

Lorne smiled. "We're getting there. Making dire progress in the process. Slowly but surely, I think we're making definite headway."

"Great, that's what I like to hear. What's in the box?" Sally walked over to the desk.

Lorne removed the lid and extracted the large pile of A4 paper. "This represents all the people who have gone missing in Norfolk over the past thirteen years."

"What? Who would have thought it? That's incredible."

"I know. Now we have a daunting task ahead of us, but I'm sure Jordan and I will break the back of it within the next few days, or possibly longer."

Sally raised a pointed finger. "Let's get one thing straight from the word go, Lorne. There are no time restraints in this department, but that's not to say we can take our foot off the gas. However, I must make it clear to you that we work differently around here. If a case needs our full attention for longer than is normally necessary, then so be it. It's more important for us to get things in order from the outset, if we don't, it could lead to a dire domino effect. That's the last thing we either want or need."

"I understand. Jordan has been brilliant. We spoke to the manager of the paint company. All we need to do now is match the information from Pickrel's schedule and the routes he took to what we have in front of us. Simple, right?"

"In theory. Do you need an extra body to help out?"

Lorne shook her head and then glanced at her partner. "Do we?"

"Nope. I think, between us, we've got this covered."

"Perfect. I knew you two would hit it off. If, however, a few days down the line, you change your mind, don't hesitate to give me a shout."

"There is something that's nibbling away at me," Lorne said hesitantly.

Sally inclined her head and gestured for her to continue. "Shoot."

"I was wondering if we should pay Pickrel a visit now."

"Get all the information you can gather together first and then, yes, I think a visit to the prison should be on your agenda. It might be good, him coming into contact with a different copper. It could have the desired effect, knock him off balance enough for you to actually get somewhere. You know what these bastards are like, they enjoy nothing more than winding up the SIO on the investigation. Throwing you into the mix might be the answer we need to really rattle his cage. Are you up for that?"

Lorne glanced sideways at her partner. "Are we?"

Jordan shrugged and then waggled his eyebrows. "Sounds great to me."

"Then yes, we're up for that. In fact, I'm looking forward to it." Lorne grinned.

"I thought you might say that. Okay, it's gone five, we're going to call it a day."

Lorne peered over her shoulder at the files vying for their attention. "Really? We were only just getting started."

"It can wait until the morning. We do nine to five, or thereabouts around here. Obviously, there will be times, you know, when we're closing in on a suspect, where it might be necessary to do a night-time surveillance, but I'm inclined to believe those will be few and far between. Let's go home and start afresh tomorrow."

Lorne shrugged. "Suits me, but just so you know, I'm willing to work longer hours when it's needed."

"I know that. Why do you think I put your name forward for the position? Anyway, you need to get back home and see to the dogs, I'm aware your work isn't finished for the day, unlike ours."

"Hopefully, Tony will have everything in hand by the time I get home."

. . .

AFTER SECURING THE ROOM, Lorne said goodbye to her new work colleagues and drove home. She found Tony up to his neck in sacks of dog food in the kennels. "Do you need a hand?" She smiled and set her bag down on the floor by the door.

"Your timing is impeccable as always. How did it go today?"

"I'll tell you over dinner. Let's feed the mutts first. Where have you got to?"

"I've done the first run. Two of them escaped the instant I opened the damn door, so I had that to deal with."

She leaned over and kissed him. "Poor baby. Why don't you leave the rest to me? What's for dinner?"

"Shit! I knew there was something else I had to do before you got home. I'll get on it right away. This lot have had me run off my feet all day, what with one thing or another. Sorry to let you down, love."

She grasped his arms that were flailing around as he spoke. "Stop! Take a breath."

He sucked in a large breath and kissed her, hard on the mouth. "I love you. Hey, and I missed having you around today, too."

Tears misted her eyes. "Oh no, don't go making me feel guilty now. I missed you and the dogs as well."

"It wasn't intentional. What do you fancy for dinner?"

"Sod it. Let's ring up for a takeaway. I know we don't have them that often."

"Phew, sounds good to me. What do you fancy?"

"I'll let you decide. I'd better get on with feeding this lot first."

"Leave it to me. I know I don't say this enough, but you're an amazing woman, Lorne Warner."

She smiled and wrinkled her nose. "Yeah, I know. Scram, let me get to work."

She watched him walk away, aware he was hobbling a little. Knowing it was pointless asking if he was all right, she made a mental note to broach the subject over dinner and turned her attention to feeding the twenty dogs they had in residence at the moment. "Hello, my pretties, have you missed me?"

TONY WAS HAVING a cuppa at the kitchen table when she finally finished the chore, thirty minutes later. She brushed down her suit and joined him at the table. He went to stand and winced.

She slapped her hand on his arm. "Stay there. I know your leg is hurting. I can make my own drink; do you want another one?"

"Yes, please. I'm sorry I've let you down today, what with this being your first day back at work."

The kettle boiled. She poured the water and a splash of milk over the coffee granules and sugar and returned to the table without replying. Handing him his mug, she kissed him and squeezed his shoulders before taking her seat opposite him. "First of all, you can pack that in, you haven't let me down. It's going to take a few days for you to get into the swing of things around here. I feel guilty for asking you to pick up where I left off. And secondly, what's wrong with your leg? I could tell it was hurting you out in the kennels. Is it bad?"

"Not really. The top aches a bit, that's all. Maybe a soak in the bath later will do it some good."

A twinkle developed in Lorne's eye. "Sounds fab to me. Want some company?"

His eyebrows rose and fell. "Now you're talking."

She fell back into her chair, laughing. "What do we have to look forward to for dinner?"

"I went for the Chinese option. I hope that's okay? It'll be here in forty minutes or so."

"Enough time for me to get changed and do a bit of housework."

"Oh no, you don't. The housework was done first thing. You could take Sheba for a run for me if you don't mind?"

"Of course." At the sound of her name, Sheba came towards Lorne and put her head on her lap. "Hey, you, I thought you were in a mood with me, not coming to greet me as soon as I walked in the door."

Her devoted German Shepherd moaned as Lorne rubbed her ears.

"Maybe she was put out that you stopped by and saw the other dogs first," Tony suggested.

"Ouch, you're probably right. She's a sensitive soul." She bent forward and kissed her on the head. Sheba moaned and tried to pull away. "Aww... you know you love your kisses."

"I'd think again about that, if that's her reaction."

Lorne picked up an apple from the fruit bowl and aimed it at him. "Smart aleck."

"Yep, that's me. How did it go at work today? Or don't you want to discuss it?"

"No, I'm fine. It's going to be a lot harder than I realised but I think I'm going to enjoy it. We still have dozens and dozens of files to go through yet, you know, from the ones that dickhead Falkirk messed up. However, Sally has got me and Jordan on the Louie Pickrel case."

"Ah, the one she used to entice you back on the force. How's it going?"

"That's the one. Jordan and I are in the process of piecing things together and then, I think a visit to see the man himself is in order. Hopefully, that is going to take place in the next few days. That reminds me, I should probably make

---

an appointment to see him with the governor first thing. It's not like I can show up at the drop of a hat."

"Yeah, very wise." Tony shuddered. "Rather you than me. I think I'd have a hard job keeping my hands off the bastard, knowing what he's got up to in the past. All those other victims yet to be discovered. I'd bloody throttle him until he confessed where he's buried the other bodies. What a sick fucker."

"I feel the same way. Going in there heavy-handed isn't going to help us. He's the type who enjoys messing with coppers' minds. We'll see how it plays out when I visit him. For now, Jordan and I are going to work hard to put all the pieces in place and hit him where it hurts, with the facts, if we can gather any."

He smiled. "I have every faith in you. The inimitable Lorne Simpkins/Warner has got this."

"I damn well hope so," she replied, less confident.

CHAPTER 3

*I*t took Lorne and Jordan two full days to gather all the information they needed to build a case against Pickrel. She had arranged to see the prisoner on Thursday at two p.m. She and Jordan were holding a meeting with Sally, where they were going over some ground rules. Sally was giving Lorne some pointers on how to handle Pickrel. She listened but had a feeling any plans they formed now would go out of the window once she was in his presence.

"So, what are we looking at, exactly?" Sally asked.

"At the moment, we have four possible victims in mind. Three girls and one boy, all aged between five and ten."

"And how have you come to this conclusion?"

Lorne faced Jordan. He urged Lorne to go ahead, appearing happy to step back out of the limelight for now. "Okay, we sourced the names off the Misper files and matched them to the routes Pickrel took during the years he was on the road as a salesman. Two of the missing children's names cropped up in a couple of the files with the dubious convictions as well. So, if we can pin the murders on Pickrel and get him to tell us where the bodies are, that's another couple of innocent people we'll be able to set free from prison."

Sally raised a finger. "Let's not jump ahead of ourselves here. You've already stated that the children are on the missing person list, but we don't know for definite that they're dead yet, do we?"

Lorne slapped herself on the wrist. "Sorry, yes, you're right. We need to get in there; we're going to take photos of the children with us. My intention is to show Pickrel the images and gauge his reaction to each one."

Sally nodded. "That's exactly how I would play it. Okay, are you still going through the files or is that you finished with the task now?"

"We've gone back over the files a few times, and nothing else is really jumping out at us, is it, Jordan?"

He shook his head. "I think we've given it our all on this one, boss. Lorne is super thorough; she doesn't discard the file until she's checked and double-checked all the facts and possibilities."

Sally beamed. "Just as I predicted. It's going to be great having you on the team, Lorne."

"One caveat to that, if I may?" Lorne said.

Sally frowned. "Go on."

"What happens when we run out of files to go over?"

Sally inhaled a large breath then let it out slowly. "I asked myself the same question when we first formed the team and, here we are, a couple of years down the line, still going through the files and earmarking some prisoners who are mistakenly sitting behind bars."

"I get that. Let's hope, over time, we can make a difference."

"We're doing that daily. Right, we've all got a lot on our plate today. I'm going to chase up the anthropologist. Simon hinted last night that she might be getting close. I thought it wouldn't hurt to test the water and give her a call. What do you think? Would you do it in my shoes, Lorne?"

"Definitely. How exciting, I can't wait to see what she comes up with. Right, Jordan and I will leave you to get on with things."

"Thanks. Stick with what you're doing, ensure you have everything to hand that you'll need for your visit to the prison."

"We're just going to go over the documents now, aren't we, Jordan?"

"If you say so." He laughed and leapt out of his chair.

"Good luck, I'll keep my fingers crossed for you." Lorne followed Jordan out of the room.

SALLY TOOK a few deep breaths and dialled the number Simon had given her. "Hello, is that Jilly?"

"It is. And who are you?"

"I'm DI Sally Parker, you're—"

"Ah, yes, I was going to give you a call later. I'm almost finished with the reconstruction. I used a laser image, it did a fabulous job, gave me an excellent foundation to work with. It was easier than I thought it was going to be, she had good bone structure still, you see. Some corpses are better than others to try to reassemble, in my experience."

"I see. I suppose I've never really thought about that before. So, do you believe it will help our investigation?"

"Let's hope so. Who knows, maybe the reconstruction will be that dire that even her own family won't recognise her. Give me another half an hour, just to make a few final tweaks and I'll deliver what I have to Simon."

"You've got it. I truly appreciate you doing this so quickly for me."

"You caught me in between jobs. No sweat, happy that I could help out."

"Thanks again. Can't wait to see it."

Sally ended the call and sat back to take it all in. She ran through what she intended to do next, regarding the investigation, her heart pounding at the knowledge that by the end of the day, she'd be a few steps closer to possibly identifying the victim. She glanced out of the window, at the grey skies over her beloved Norfolk for a second or two and then got back to the paperwork she needed to attend to for headquarters. More rules and regulation adjustments, it was a nightmare trying to keep up with the changes in policies; most of her colleagues were saying the same nowadays. *Why can't they get things right in the first place, rather than mess us around like this? Bloody pen-pushers with nothing better to do, I shouldn't wonder.*

At FIVE O'CLOCK, Sally received the call she'd been waiting for from Simon. "It's here. Do you want to drop by now or wait until the morning to see it?"

"No way! You just try and stop me seeing it tonight, I'm leaving now." She didn't give Simon a chance to reply, she slammed the phone down and shot out of her chair and whooped for joy.

When she entered the outer office, the rest of the team were staring at her. "Sorry about that, my enthusiasm got the better of me. The reconstruction is now complete. I'm going over to the mortuary to see it. You guys can finish up here for the night, I'll bring you up to date first thing in the morning. I love it when a plan comes together. Jack, do you want to come with me or are you going to head home?"

He cringed. "Would you mind if I give it a miss, boss?

70

Donna has got something planned for tonight with the girls, I told her I'd be home early."

Sally waved her hand. "It's fine. Go." Sally's gaze turned directly to the desk next to him, and she found Lorne beaming at her. "Are you up for it, Lorne?"

"I thought you'd never ask."

"Great. Be ready to leave in five. I've just got to tidy up my desk before I switch off the light."

A few minutes later, the outer office was empty, except for Lorne who was standing, waiting by the door.

"I'm super excited to see what the victim looks like, aren't you?" Sally said, joining her.

"Definitely. It's going to be brilliant for you if you can get the ball rolling on the case and let the family know she's been found."

"Yeah, I suppose that's going to be the tough part. I'll deal with that tomorrow. Let's go. Do you want to follow me in your car, the mortuary is on the way home anyway?"

"Makes sense to me."

They wound their way down the concrete stairs, bid the desk sergeant, Pat, farewell for the evening and jumped in their respective cars.

Sally put her foot down and grinned as she saw Lorne keep up with her in the rear-view mirror. In no time at all, they were parking their cars in the few vacant spaces outside the mortuary. They raced through the corridor to Simon's office. He greeted them and showed them into another room. There, protected by a crisp white sheet, was the reconstructed head of the victim. Simon carefully removed the covering and Sally and Lorne both gasped.

"My God, that's simply amazing. And for Jilly to create something so beautiful, in the amount of time we gave her, is well, simply phenomenal," Sally gushed.

"I agree. It's outstanding. The detail is exceptional," Lorne whispered.

"Yep, she's remarkable. That's why I use her," Simon said, grinning like a child at his first football game.

Although the reconstruction was good, Sally wasn't so naïve as to consider it to be one hundred percent accurate, but in her mind, there would be enough for her to match to a victim's photo, should the woman be lingering in any of their files. "I can't say I recognise her from any of the cases I've sifted through over the years. What about you, Lorne? You've been the one searching through the files over the past few days."

"Some of them, not all of them. Maybe she's in one of the files where the offender has died during their sentence."

"There is that. We'll check in the morning. For now, I think I can rest easier, knowing that we're on the right track. If nothing shows up in the files then I'll be calling on the media and the general public for their help."

"It's a start, like you say," Lorne agreed. "It's more than we had this morning, that's for certain."

"Yep."

"Right, ladies, I can't stand around here, I need to drop by the supermarket on the way home before my tyrant of a wife nails my arse to the wall," Simon announced loudly, almost scaring the shit out of Sally who was standing close to him.

She swiped him on the arm, hard. "Jesus, I was lost in thought and you do that to me. And yes, you'd better get your skates on, I'm starving."

The three of them laughed.

After Sally snapped off a couple of photos with her phone, she and Lorne left Simon to lock up and made their way back to their cars. "Do you want me in earlier in the morning?" Lorne asked, the eagerness in her eyes telling

Sally she'd made the right choice bringing her back to the world of policing.

"No, make it the usual time. I won't be there until nine. I think we've both given the force more free hours than we care to mention over the years. Let's stick to our proper hours, for the time being, at least."

"I knew there was a reason I was going to enjoy working under you, my friend. I'll see you tomorrow then. Have a good evening, I hope Simon manages to snag something nice for you at the supermarket. You lucky thing."

"Won't Tony have dinner ready and waiting for you by the time you get home?"

"If last night's shenanigans are anything to go by, I doubt it. We ended up making the takeaway richer."

"Oh dear. I suppose he has his hands full, caring for the dogs all day."

"Yeah, he needs to get into a routine. That's never really been high up on his agenda. It's not part of MI6's training, I wish it was."

"You two make the perfect team. I'm sure you'll work it out within a few days. Enjoy your evening, Lorne."

"You, too, Sally."

Lorne jumped in her car and drove off. Sally watched her go, proud to have her as a close friend and an efficient member of her Cold Case Unit.

CHAPTER 4

The team gathered the following morning. Sally downloaded the photos she'd taken and asked Jack to put them up on the fifty-inch TV screen on the wall. Everyone gasped when the reconstruction appeared, just like Sally and Lorne had the evening before.

"That's amazing," Joanna muttered.

Jordan shuddered and mumbled, "I think it's a little eerie, but that might just be me."

"There's definitely an air of mystique around it," Stuart agreed. "I wouldn't call it eerie, though, mate."

"Each to their own," Jordan countered.

"Okay, what we're going to need to do first is go over the files again. Lorne doesn't think she recognises the woman from the files she and Jordan have been working on lately, so that definitely narrows things down a touch."

"I agree," Jordan said.

"So, we've got the older files to sift through. I'm going to do that with Jack this morning."

"Oh, the joys of being the guv's partner," Jack grumbled good-naturedly, and the others laughed.

"He loves me really. Right, so it's as we were yesterday with the rest of the tasks. Lorne and Jordan, where are you up to on the Pickrel case?"

"We've got the possible identities of four victims so far and an appointment this afternoon with Pickrel. I thought we'd continue going over the files we have, just to make sure we haven't missed anything. I could check through the missing persons list for the Jane Doe at the same time, if you want me to?"

"Yes, if you would. The sooner we get her identified, the better."

After another round of coffee, they got down to work.

Sally began sifting through the files they had set aside with Jack. "You take that pile and I'll go through these. Look thoroughly, Jack, don't just discard them willy-nilly."

Jack stared at her open-mouthed for a moment. "Hey, as if I would."

A couple of hours later, Sally punched the air. "Yes, yes, yes. I think I've found her."

Jack stood behind her and looked over her shoulder as she compared the woman's photo she'd plucked from a file to the reconstruction she'd brought up on her phone.

"There's no doubt in my mind," Jack announced.

Sally called Lorne over to take a look. "What do you think?"

Lorne sighed resignedly. "Yep, I think you've just found your victim."

"Okay, looking at the file, the suspect was a Gordon Dawson. He was arrested and charged with killing two women. Both bodies were found in the undergrowth in a park close to his home around twelve years ago. Which matches to what Simon reckons about the victim—he told me he thought she'd lost her life between ten and fifteen years ago."

"Hmm… different MO, unless the other victims were found buried," Lorne stated.

Sally shook her head. "Nope, they were found in the open, hidden behind bushes." She flipped through the pages to Dawson's interview notes. "Hmm… he's always denied killing anyone else."

"Jesus, so Falkirk went ahead and stitched him up. Thought it was better to pin this victim on Dawson, rather than having another missing person not accounted for. What a sick shit he was." Jack shook his head in disgust.

"So it would seem. We're all agreed then, this is Jackie Swan?"

"Yep, if you still have any doubts in your mind, maybe run it past Simon first, before you contact the family."

Sally winked at Lorne. "Good idea." She rang her husband's mobile. "Sorry to bother you, just a quickie. We think we've identified the Jane Doe. If I send you her photo, can you have a look for me, see what you think, before I set off to speak to the family?"

"Of course I will. Send it over while I'm on the phone."

"Hang tight, doing it now… Sent. Have you got it?"

Simon paused for a few seconds. His phone pinged at the other end. "Here it is now. Give me a second. I'll go in the other room and pick out some of the features in her face, see if they match the reconstruction."

"Okay. Sounds like a plan to me."

Footsteps sounded, and a door squeaked open. His breathing quickened as he compared the image to what he had in front of him. "Right, all done. I'm happy for you to go ahead. I believe they are the same person. Well done you for solving the case so quickly."

"Hold your horses. I wouldn't be so quick as to say we've *solved* it just yet. We found the victim in the dubious pile."

"I'm not with you. Care to explain?"

"All right. We're looking through the Falkirk cold cases, the ones he mishandled. We have a pile where the persons who were charged with the crimes have either died in prison, or since been released, having served the sentence for a crime they were innocent of. In this case, Gordon Dawson died in prison a couple of years ago."

"Ah, I see. Which means you won't be able to question him further."

"Exactly. In my mind, the MOs are different and therefore it was an unsafe conviction."

He sucked in a breath. "I'd be careful taking that route, Sal."

"May I ask why?"

"If you're going to open a can of worms, you're going to put the family through hell all over again."

"I get that. On the other hand, if I don't investigate it thoroughly, it means there could still be a murderer out there who has been free for the past twelve years."

Simon heaved out another sigh. "You do have a point. All right, I would still tread carefully. Twelve years is an awfully long time to start dredging up old feelings again. To cause a family more turmoil than they need, all these years later."

"I know. I'll be careful and sensitive, I promise. I'm going to share the reconstruction with them, is that okay?"

"Go for it. I wouldn't necessarily go in there and show it to them first of all, though, maybe ease it into the conversation after a few minutes of getting to know the family."

"No, really?" She laughed. "Grant me with some common sense, husband dearest."

"Sorry, I forgot who I was talking to then. You'll be surprised how many times I have to state the obvious to other serving officers. Please accept my apologies."

"I can imagine. No apology needed. I'll let you know how I get on later."

"Before you go, Sal. The man who was convicted of the crime, did he admit to it at the time? Was it police coercion?"

"Nope, he's always denied it. Hang on, let me check the end of the file." Sally read the summary notes from the prison, and a lump appeared in her throat. She coughed to clear it. "Shit! He even denied it on his deathbed. In tears and with his dying breath, he admitted to killing the two women he was convicted for, but flat-out denied killing anyone else."

"That's so sad. What did he have to lose by lying?"

"Nothing. Damn, okay, now I feel sorry for a killer, is that wrong of me?"

"No. That's because you're a kind and loving person. See you later."

"Thanks for that. Bye for now."

Sally ended the call and faced Lorne. "He's agreed and given me the go-ahead to speak to the family."

"You sound as though you still have some doubts," Lorne said.

"I suppose I have. On the one hand, I think we're doing the right thing going to see the family, however, on the other, as Simon just reminded me, we'll be pulling off a plaster that has probably healed old wounds. If you get what I mean by that. I'm not sure how else to put it, not really."

"I understand where you're coming from. You just need to go and see them, see where the land lies first and go from there."

"You're right, of course. Come on, Jack, let's get this over with."

"Hang on. Do we know where we're even going?"

"Damn. No. The family might have moved by now. Time to take a step back and do some more digging. See, I'm racing ahead before I've got all the pertinent facts in front of me. I know, don't say it, I need to calm down and assess things thoroughly first, otherwise I could end up with egg on my face, right?"

Jack grinned. "You took the words out of my mouth."

Lorne held out a piece of paper for Sally to take. "This might help."

Sally took the sheet and read it. She looked up at Lorne and shook her head. "You're amazing."

"I'm not, not really. All I did was delve deeper while you were on the phone to Simon. We had all the missing person cases from thirteen years ago to hand. I just located the appropriate file while you were distracted."

"I appreciate it, Lorne. Thank you. I'll get on the system, see if the husband is still at the same address. Unless there's a mobile number on here."

Lorne pointed halfway down the sheet. "It's there."

Sally smiled. "Great stuff. I'll call him from my office."

Jack followed her out of the room, where the dubious files were sitting, and Sally returned to her office to make the call. Her fingers were slippery with sweat as she rang Robert Swan's number. The phone was answered after a couple of rings by a female.

"Hello, sorry to trouble you. I was after a Robert Swan, is this still his number?"

"It is. Who are you?"

"I'm DI Sally Parker from the Norfolk Constabulary."

"Oh, I see. Yes, okay. I'll get him for you, he's in the loo at the moment."

"Thanks, I'll hold." Too much information there, thanks all the same. Phew! At least I have the correct number.

Sally drummed her fingers on the desk until Robert Swan came on the line a little while later.

"Hello, this is Robert Swan. What's this about?"

"Hello, Mr Swan. I'm DI Sally Parker. I wondered if it would be convenient to drop by and see you sometime today."

"For what reason, may I ask?"

Sally chewed on her lip for a second or two. "Umm… we believe there's been a development in your wife's case?"

"My wife? What are you talking about? Serena, this officer says it's to do with you. What in God's name have you been up to?"

"No, no. I'm sorry. I should correct myself and say it's your former wife, Jackie, I was referring to."

"Oh, I'm with you now. A development you say? In the form of what?"

"I'd rather we discuss that in person, sir, if that's all right with you?"

"Do I have a choice? My wife has been dead for twelve years, a man was convicted of her murder, and now you're on the phone, hinting at some sort of development. You'll have to forgive my confusion."

"All will become clear when we meet up. Are you free today, sir?"

"Yes, my *current* wife, sorry, is that the right term? I don't know. Anyway, Serena and I were planning on going out for dinner later, but we're chilling by the pool for now."

It was Sally's turn to be confused, and she checked outside the window to see if the sun had come out since she had arrived at work. It hadn't. It was still damp and dreary. "Sorry, are you here, in Norfolk, or abroad at the moment?"

"In Norfolk, at home. Ah, I get what you're on about. Sorry, we have an indoor pool."

Sally smiled. "Ah, that explains it. Okay, is it still the same address or have you moved?"

"No, I left the old house about a year after Jackie disappeared. I couldn't stand being in the place any longer, not with all the good memories we had there. It felt empty and just wrong, being there."

"Understandable. Can I have your new address, sir?"

"Yes, it's Brightwater House, Simnel Drive, Acle."

"Okay. It'll take us a good half an hour to get there."

"We'll get dressed then. See you soon."

BRIGHTWATER HOUSE COULD ONLY BE DESCRIBED as fantabulous in Sally's eyes. She thought her mansion was lovely, but in all honesty, it was a poor relative in comparison to what was laid out before her. As soon as they turned the corner and saw the massive locked gates, Jack let out a low whistle.

"Bugger me! I sense this place is going to be humungous. At least a couple of mill, easily, not that we can see much from the road."

"You're not kidding. Can you recall what he does for a living?"

"I can't, sorry. I can remember his old address, though, and it wasn't in as classy a neighbourhood as this one."

"Strange. Maybe he won a pot of money on the lottery then. It doesn't really matter. Do me a favour, brave the rain and announce our arrival, will you?"

"Is that you delegating when it suits again?"

Sally beamed and wrinkled her nose at her partner. He pulled the collar of his jacket up around his neck and left the warmth of the car. Jack pushed the buzzer and spoke into the microphone, situated at head height on the wall, alongside the black wrought-iron gates. Then he trotted back to the car as the rain hammered the windscreen.

The gates opened to reveal a white and glass box of a building that appeared to have come straight out of a *Grand Designs* programme. "Jesus, it's huge and such an individual-looking house. If you can call it a house," Sally enthused.

"It's all right, if you're into this type of property. It doesn't ring my bell in the slightest. Too poncey and show-offy for my taste," Jack grumbled.

Sally approached the house slowly, in awe of its presence within the immaculate grounds. "That's just jealousy on your part."

"Is it heck? Why would you want to live in a box with a flat roof? You know those things are prone to leaking, don't you?"

"Not on something like this, I bet. Any misapprehension about leaky roofs would have been covered at the planning stage."

"Whatever. It just doesn't appeal to me. Anyway, time is getting on, and we're not here to admire the lousy architecture, we're here to break the bad news about his wife, aren't we?"

"You really can be such a miserable fucker at times, Jack Blackman. Beautiful architecture needs to be studied and appreciated."

"Yeah, and that's where we differ. Mind you, your father is a builder and property developer, so I suppose you have to have a certain amount of interest in the subject."

"Correction. Both Dad and Simon are property developers, and yes, it helps to show an interest in what keeps bringing the money in. But even if they weren't, who in their right mind, if money wasn't an object, wouldn't want to own a house of this stature and magnificence?"

Jack shook his head. "All right, you can stop drooling now. I'd like to get home today, if at all possible."

"Sourpuss. A jealous one at that."

"Bollocks."

Sally got out of the car, too engrossed in her surroundings to be bothered if she got wet or not. It was Jack pushing her in the back, urging her to get under the cover of the expansive porch that brought her out of her flabbergasted state.

"Are you mad? Look at you, you're drenched."

"Oops, so I am. I bet they have super-duper heating to combat that inside, so I should dry out in a few seconds."

"What planet are you from again? Who are you? What have you done with my usually utilitarian boss?"

Sally grinned. "Has anyone ever told you how cute you are when you're vexed?"

He stood there and stared at her for a few seconds then let out an exasperated breath and rang the bell which echoed around the inside of the house.

It took a while for the door to be opened. Standing on the doorstep, with a glimpse of the magnificence of what was to come hitting them over his shoulder, was who Sally presumed to be Robert Swan. *Unless they have a butler!*

"Hello, you must be the officer who rang me earlier. Sorry, I've forgotten your name already, I've got a head like a sieve at the best of times."

"That's right, Mr Swan." Sally produced her warrant card and thrust it under his nose. "I'm DI Sally Parker, and this is my partner, DS Jack Blackman."

"I'm pleased to meet you. I suppose you'd better come in. We're through here, in the lounge."

Sally paused before she took a step into the sparkling marble-floored hallway. "Would you prefer it if we removed our shoes? The weather is ghastly today."

He motioned for them to follow him. "There's really no

need for that. Come through, we've just lit the fire, so it should help you dry off."

Jack closed the front door behind them. If Sally thought the entrance hall was incredible, it truly wasn't anything compared to what lay ahead of them. At one end of the room was a full-sized library with what appeared to be first-edition books. It had a roving ladder tucked up in the far corner, every child's dream to climb as a kid. A woman with shoulder-length blonde hair, wearing the smartest velour casual lounge suit she'd ever seen, was sitting in one of the two Queen Anne armchairs positioned on either side of the inglenook fireplace. Robert Swan had already hinted that the fire would be roaring and he was right, it was in full flow, consisting of six to eight logs, all glowing fiercely at the heart of the opening. The heat hit them the farther they moved into the room. Just beyond the armchairs were a couple of white leather couches, facing one another.

Robert pointed at one of them. "Please, take a seat."

The three of them sat, Jack and Sally on the right-hand couch, and Robert chose to sit alongside his wife, close to the fire.

"I'll sit here for now, until it becomes unbearable. Perhaps you'd like to tell me what this visit is about? You mentioned it was to do with my former wife. I must say, I was somewhat perplexed by your call."

"Now, Robert, where are your manners?" the blonde said. "I'm Serena, by the way, or should I say Mrs Swan. Can I get either of you a drink of tea or coffee?" The largest of smiles forced her ruby-coloured lips apart. "Or something stronger perhaps?"

Sally held up a hand before Jack could jump in and say something. "We're fine. We wouldn't want to put you out."

"Good, can we please get on with it? My inquisitorial gene is playing havoc with my thoughts," Robert insisted.

"Then I won't keep you in suspense any longer. A few days ago, a skeleton was discovered at Thompson Common. We believe the remains are those of your missing wife, or should I say, your former wife."

Robert's eyes widened, and he flung himself back into his chair. "What? It can't be. No, not after all this time."

Serena let out a gasp. She flew out of her chair and dropped to her knees on the floor beside her husband.

"There's no doubt in either our minds or the pathologist's."

Robert ran a hand over his face and dragged it through his hair. "I don't understand. How can you tell? It's been twelve years since she went missing and that man was sentenced for her murder, I dread to think what state the remains were in. Oh shit! I feel sick."

"I'm sorry to put you through this trauma, I truly am. Yes, you're right, your wife's remains were nothing more than a skeleton, although some buttons and parts of her shoes were also found with her. We can look at those further down the line if you think you'll be able to recognise them."

"What are you saying? That you want me to look at her skeleton and identify her?"

"No, I apologise for misleading you. We've already identified your wife, sorry, former wife, by carrying out a facial reconstruction."

He stared at Sally. "Like a mould, the type you see on TV sometimes?"

"That's right. The anthropologist was able to use lasers to create the image and formed the mould from the details she captured. Would you like to see it? I have a photo on my phone."

"Do I have to? I mean, well, is it bad? Will it make me vomit? Because I'm on the verge of doing just that right now."

"I don't think it's bad. In fact, I think it's remarkable, but then, she was a stranger to me, not a member of my family, so I can't truly predict how you will feel." Sally's gaze drifted to Serena who was staring at her husband, rubbing a hand over his. She, too, looked astonished by what she'd heard.

"What do you think, Serena, should we take a look? You knew her as well as I did. Will we be able to handle this, after all these years?"

"You knew her?" Sally interrupted.

Serena faced her with tears in her eyes and nodded. "Jackie was my best friend."

"Ah, I see. I wasn't aware of that. I should have reacquainted myself in detail with the case before coming here today. And you two are now married?"

They clutched hold of each other's hands and smiled.

"Yes, we had to wait a few years to make it official," Robert said, not taking his eyes off his adoring wife.

"Ah yes. The wait must have been tough for you both?" Sally asked, keeping her smile set in place.

Robert nodded. "It was, although it never stopped us from moving in together. There was no law preventing us from doing that."

"Of course there isn't. You understand why the law is in place, though, don't you?"

Robert glanced at Sally and frowned. "I'm not an imbecile, Inspector. Before you come in here casting aspersions on our behaviour, maybe you'd care to take a step back and put yourself in our position, or in *my* position, at least. My wife went missing at night, the coppers back in the day were less than useless, then out of the blue we hear that man had been arrested and was a suspected serial killer, and yet he refused to tell the inspector investigating our case where he'd buried her body."

86

"I'm aware of that much. There's something else I need to tell you."

Robert removed his hands from his wife's and swivelled in his seat to face Sally. "Go on, I'm all ears, hanging on to your every word."

His sarcasm wasn't lost on Sally. Maybe she should have gone over the file more thoroughly before showing up here. "Our team was created a few years ago because the inspector who initially dealt with your case was suspended for dubious behaviour."

Serena left her place on the floor and dashed back to her chair.

"What? What are you saying? Go on, come right out and tell me in layman's terms, if you would?" Robert asked.

Sally inhaled and let the breath seep through her lips. "We are dealing with over a hundred cases where we believe the wrong people were convicted for the crimes."

"Is this for real? How the fucking hell can that happen?" He shook his head in utter disbelief.

"We're not sure. I simply don't have all the answers for you, I'm afraid. The thing is, when Gordon Dawson was arrested and convicted of your wife's murder, he always denied it."

Robert pointed. "See, this is where things get really screwed up for me. I always thought at the time it was reckless to convict the man, you know, without the body. How often does that happen? Is it even ethical to do such a thing?"

Sally contemplated what to say next. "Between you and me, it rarely happens. I have known a person to be convicted over the years when the evidence against them has been hard to dismiss. But they've always been what I class as 'safe convictions'."

"No turning back convictions, nailed-on certainties, is that right?"

"Yes, that's correct. Furthermore, when I dug into Dawson's prison record, at the time of his death, actually on his deathbed, he again categorically stressed that he did not kill your wife."

"I can't believe I'm hearing this. Jesus, how to rip someone's world apart within ten minutes of meeting them."

"I'm sorry, that truly wasn't my intention."

"So, what was your intention, Inspector? I'm waiting with bated breath to hear."

"I suppose to give you and the other members of your family closure. You've waited twelve years to hear the news. Yes, okay, you've moved on with your life, but I'm wagering that you've always had a niggling doubt in your mind as to what happened to your wife and whether she was likely to show up. She was reported as a missing person after all, am I right?"

"Yes, of course you are. Like I said, Serena and I never stopped expecting her to walk back into our lives. We were drawn together through the trauma, the impact of the situation. In fact, we often discuss Jackie, don't we, love?"

Serena offered a weak smile. "We do. She was a massive part of both of our lives, it would be immoral of us not to. We both loved her very much. I really don't know how I feel, you being here today, sharing this news with us."

"Our intentions are all good, I assure you. Nevertheless, it is our responsibility to revisit the case."

"What? Why?" Tension wrinkled and contorted Robert's expression.

"Firstly, it's what we do when a body surfaces like this and, secondly, we believe Dawson was innocent and DI Falkirk fitted him up for the crime. Therefore, it's our responsibility to uncover the truth."

"I get that, but what use will it be, we're still talking about twelve years later here."

"It really doesn't matter how long has passed. Think of it this way, for twelve years the real killer has been walking free. Who knows what they've been up to in that time and how many more people they have killed?"

"Jesus, that thought never even crossed my mind," Robert said. He fell silent to contemplate the situation for a few moments and then asked, "I don't suppose there is any doubt that she was murdered, is there? What I suppose I'm asking is, how did she die? Can you even tell that sort of thing?"

"It's surprising what a skeletal discovery can tell us. Sorry, first of all, before we go any further, why don't I show you the reconstruction?"

Robert glanced at Serena and asked, "Are you ready for this?"

Serena swallowed loudly, and the colour in her cheeks drained before their eyes. "I think so, although I'm not a hundred percent sure. It's going to be weird seeing her after all these years."

"I agree." He reached out a hand for hers and then turned his attention back to Sally once more. "Okay, we're ready."

Sally enlarged the photo on her phone then stood to reveal the image to the couple. Robert was the first to gasp.

In a whisper, he said, "Jesus, there's no doubt in my mind. Serena, what about you?"

Serena recoiled from the image and closed her eyes. Tears oozed from her tightly shut eyes. "Please, take it away."

Robert left his seat to comfort his wife, and Sally returned to the sofa. "I'm sorry. It was never my intention to cause you any distress."

Robert hugged his wife. "We have to think of this as constructive. Knowing that Jackie could have been still out there has haunted us for years, you know it has, love. We need to see this as a positive outcome—maybe that's the wrong term to use. Help me out here, Inspector, I know what I want to say but I'm failing to express it effectively."

"Outcome, or result, either or. The main issue is that we have discovered Jackie's body. All we need to do now is track down her killer. Someone buried her body in that grave, we need to find out who that person was and to punish them, through the system, for killing her and leaving her body to rot in that grave for twelve years."

"I agree. The sooner that happens the better in my eyes, too. One question, how was she discovered? Why now, after all these years?"

"As I said, Jackie's skeleton was dug up at Thompson Common. They're in the process of thinning out the forest down there, ridding it of all the trees that have perished over the years and replacing them with saplings. It was during this process, with the diggers in full flow, that the workmen uncovered the remains. Work was halted immediately, allowing the pathologist and SOCO to take over."

"I still can't believe it's true, after all these years. My emotions are topsy-turvy. What happened, back in the day, has come rushing back and is now settled in my mind. I haven't revisited that night in years," Robert told them, his voice cracking a little.

"How do you feel about going over what happened that night? No pressure, not today, but soon," Sally asked.

His mouth turned down at the sides. "I suppose, if you're intent on reopening the case, now is as good a time as any."

"It'll really help. Do you want to do this separately?"

He shrugged. "I don't mind. You want to go over our statements, what we told the police at the time, is that it?"

"More about what you can remember. I don't mind Serena being here, but it's up to you. I appreciate this is going to bring back all manner of emotions for you, something you both need to prepare yourselves for."

"I'm all right to continue as we are. How about you, Serena?"

She gave her husband a weak smile. "I'm easy with it. Maybe I should make us all a drink first, what do you think?"

"Inspector? Sergeant?" Robert asked.

"Okay, you've twisted our arms. Thank you, white, one sugar for both of us." Sally could feel Jack's glare in the back of her head. *I'm only thinking about his arteries. He'll thank me eventually.*

Serena smiled and left the room. She closed the glass doors behind her. Jack took out his notebook in readiness for what Robert was about to tell them. "In your own time, Mr Swan," Sally asked.

"Please, it's Robert."

"Thank you. Begin when you're ready."

"We started out that evening in a good mood. We were all at a party at a mutual friend's house. He and his wife were celebrating their tenth wedding anniversary. Everything was going well until Jackie had a bit too much to drink. She was getting loud, wanted to leave, reluctantly I suggested we should leave for the night. She even upset Serena here, didn't she, love?" He glanced up as his wife entered the room with a tray of drinks.

"Sorry, what have I missed?"

"I was going through what happened that night. Told the officers that Jackie was getting loud because of the drink she'd consumed. She upset you before we left, didn't she?"

"Sort of. Back in the day, I was touchy about my weight. She peed me off, told me I should eat more and if I put on weight, I could always buy a pair of bigger jeans. That didn't go down too well with me."

"Oh dear. That's a cardinal rule, isn't it?" Sally smiled. "Never discuss your weight with someone else."

"Yep. I'm a different person these days. Back then I was

91

totally insecure." She reached out and held Robert's hand. "Robert has changed me for the better."

Sally smiled. "May I ask when you two got together?"

Robert's gaze dropped to the fawn-coloured deep-pile carpet, and he gulped. "It was around two years after Jackie went missing."

"Yes, that's right. We supported each other. I was going through a rough patch in my marriage at the time. You see, Jackie was my best friend. It devastated me when she went missing. Robert and I were out there day and night looking for her for the first month or so. She didn't contact us at all, either of us. It was a surprise when that inspector informed us that man had been arrested and later charged with her murder. Are you telling us that the inspector beat a confession out of him?"

Sally tutted and twisted her lips. "I can neither deny nor confirm the details of us revisiting the investigations and arrests he made. All my team are trying to do is right the wrongs that have taken place over the years in this area."

"Quite right, too," Serena said.

"But, if he didn't kill Jackie, you're going to have a nigh impossible task on your hands finding the real killer, after all these years," Robert suggested.

Sally smiled. "I have a brilliant team of investigators around me. If the killer is still out there, we will track them down. However, we're going to need to revisit and speak to all the witnesses and friends and family who were questioned at the time of Jackie's disappearance. Can you tell me what happened when you left the party? Sorry, where was the party being held?"

"It was at Alan and Anna Wakes' house, over in Holt. We lived a couple of miles from them at the time. I drove home that night, and with about a mile to go, I ran out of petrol. I'd foolishly forgotten to fill up on the way back from work and when I checked in the boot, the spare petrol can wasn't there. I also messed up with my mobile; I forgot to charge that before we attended the party. It was a culmination of screw-ups that evening. I told Jackie to come with me. I was concerned the road was pitch-black and we'd broken down on the corner. I warned her that someone might come along and crash into the back of us. Never in my wildest dreams did I ever think someone would show up there and kidnap her, or she would leave the car under her own steam. That's what we thought at the time, that she had run off and left me."

"Why would you think that? Was your marriage in trouble?"

The couple looked at each other again.

A few seconds later, Robert answered, "Yes, we didn't have the happiest of marriages, but we were working through our problems."

"How long had there been problems between you?" Sally probed.

"I suppose a couple of years."

"When you say you were working through your problems, or trying to, can you tell us what that entailed?"

Robert frowned. "If you're asking if we were visiting a counsellor, then no, we hadn't considered doing that. We were both too busy at the time."

Sally resisted the temptation to glance around the sumptuous interior again. "What careers did both of you have back then?"

"She was an estate agent, and I was an accounts manager for an import business."

"It obviously pays well," she said with a smile.

"It has its moments. Ah, I see where this is leading now, you're wondering where all of this came from, yes?"

Sally nodded. "I'm the inquisitive type."

"There was a slight insurance payout after my wife went missing and the conviction came through, of around two hundred grand, give or take a few pounds. But all of this came to us courtesy of a premium bonds win a couple of years ago. I invested some of the money from the insurance, fifty grand, the max we could invest, and bingo, within six months we'd hit the jackpot. We're still stunned about living here. We were totally out of our comfort zone when we first moved in, weren't we, love?"

Serena nodded and smiled. "I should say. I'm still not used to calling this place home yet. It's taking us a while to furnish it, we've still got a couple of the six bedrooms to kit out yet."

"I can imagine. It's a very grand house. Not sure what I would do with a million pounds if it fell into my lap. Congratulations by the way."

"And before you ask, I wanted to share it with my family, but they insisted we should keep it, invest it in property instead," Robert added.

"That makes perfect sense to me. So, if we can go back to the night... of the party, Serena, did you stay at the Wakes' house?"

"Yes. I continued to mingle with our friends."

"Did anyone else leave soon after Robert and Jackie?"

She paused to recall that night. Her brow furrowed as she thought. Eventually, she shook her head. "I don't think so, there again, I can't really be certain, not after all this time. I'm sorry."

"Don't be. I know I was asking the impossible. Was there any sign of a struggle in the car when you returned, Robert?"

"No, not as far as I could tell, and I can't honestly remember what the police report said at the time."

"I'll take a look when we get back to the station. We'll also request the forensic files from back then as well. I don't recall seeing those in the file, can you, DS Blackman?"

Jack frowned. "No, I can't say I can. I'll make a note of that."

"You say you searched for Jackie for months. Did you ever hear of any sightings of her in that time?"

"No, we heard nothing. That was the frustrating part. Which led me to believe she had been taken rather than she just upped and left me. Why would she have done that in the dead of the night in the middle of nowhere?"

"Did the police take the investigation seriously at the time?"

"I thought so. But you being here has caused me to have serious doubts now. Do you think if that prat had investigated the case properly, she would have been found sooner? Either dead or alive?"

Sally sighed and shrugged. "Unfortunately, there's no way of telling if that might have been the case. All we can do is revisit what happened that night, see if anything pokes at us to investigate further. It might not do, and there's a distinct possibility that we might end up going round and round in circles, we'll need to be prepared for that. But with your help, we'd at least try to give it a go now that Jackie's body has been found."

"Yes, yes. Please, just because I have moved on with my life, I would still very much like to know how and why this happened. As far as I know, there were no signs of danger in the area at the time."

"By that you mean, no warnings in the press or on the news, telling women to be careful?"

"That's right. You get them now and again when there's a dangerous criminal on the loose targeting women, don't you?"

"Yes, we have been known to draw on the press and TV stations to issue those types of warnings over the years. Had there been anything around that time, I take it you wouldn't have left her there, alone in the car?"

"Too bloody right. After she went missing, I found it impossible to sleep for almost two weeks. Serena will back me up here. We were out there looking, day and night, that's right, isn't it, love?" He took a sip from his drink.

"Yes, it was heartbreaking. A part of my life I will never forget. Knowing that she was out there somewhere and unable to get back to us. We had no idea what torment, or indeed torture, she was possibly going through. She had no reason to just up and leave like that." She glanced down at the cup she was holding and then looked up at Sally and continued, "Robert loved her, like he said, they were making the most of their marriage and trying to work things out. Jackie liked her drink, maybe she was too far gone that night to retaliate when someone took her from the car. I don't know, it's just something that has been going around in my head for years. Could either of us have done better that night for her?" She shrugged and let out a shuddering breath. "I can't say. Neither of us can. Hindsight is a wonderful thing, but not always helpful in these situations."

"That's a true statement. Robert, when you were driving home that night, did you notice a car following you?" Sally also took a sip from her mug.

"No, not at all. Do you really think I would have left her there, alone, if I had?"

"Sorry, I guess not. That stretch of road, is it usually busy?" Sally asked, undeterred by his terse response.

"Not really. Just like any other country road around these parts, I suppose it has its busy spells during the day, when people are going to and from work maybe."

"Okay, going back to the party, did your wife fall out with anyone that night?"

"Nope, nothing like that. She was slightly intoxicated and

loud, whether someone had an issue with that, I wouldn't know. No one came right out and said anything at the time."

"Can you tell me if all the partygoers were questioned back then?"

"Not sure about on the night, but I think they were all spoken to within a few days. I don't think we can fault the police there."

"What about in her job, could she have fallen out with anyone at work in the weeks leading up to her disappearance?"

"Not that I was aware of. Grant, her boss, was there at the party that night."

"Did he speak to your wife?"

"Yes, for a while. They got on well together. He was part of our little gang, I suppose you would call it."

"Is he still around?"

"Yes, he runs the Millmart's Estate Agent and is still part of our friendship ring. We're all still really good friends, even if some of them objected to Serena and me getting together."

Sally inclined her head. "Really? Why would anyone object to that?"

His shoulder hitched a little. "Not sure. Serena was there every step of the way when I needed her. I used to ring her late at night, not once did she turn her back on me."

"And you were married at the time, Serena, is that right?"

"Yes. And before you ask, yes, it did piss Denis off. But my marriage wasn't worth saving anyway. He'd had countless affairs over the years, it was only a matter of time before we drifted apart. Maybe Jackie going missing was the final nail in the coffin." She winced and squeezed her eyes shut. "Damn, sorry, maybe that was the wrong thing to say in the circumstances."

"I understand what you mean," Sally replied. "It pushed you both to realise the marriage wasn't working."

"Yes, that's it in a nutshell. And before you ask, there was nothing going on between Robert and me at the time. She was my best friend, I would never have done anything to have harmed our friendship in any way."

"Good to know. So the shock, and you working together to try to find Jackie, were the contributing factors for you two finally getting together, I take it?"

"Yes, that's it. It took us a while to fall in love with each other. We did it for the right reasons though in the end," Serena stated, smiling at her husband and squeezing his hand tighter.

"Okay, well, I think we've covered everything we need to, for now. I'm going to leave you one of my cards. Please ring me if there's anything else you can think of that you believe will help the case."

"What are you going to do now?" Robert asked.

"Today's visit was all about us telling you that we had discovered your wife's remains and that we were reopening the case into her death. We're going to go back to the station and familiarise ourselves with the facts of the case. Draw up a list of people we'd like to question and go from there. Perhaps you can tell me if all your friends are still living in the area?"

"As far as I know," Robert said. "Those who objected to us getting together have drifted apart over the years, it's what people do, isn't it?"

"There comes a time in our lives when yes, we have to move on. Do you know if they all live at the same addresses?"

He thought it over for a second or two, and Serena nodded. "Yes, we think so. If you have any problems, we can give you everyone's mobile number, people don't tend to change them."

"That would be helpful. We'll get back to you on that if we need them."

Sensing that Sally was about to leave, Jack closed his notebook. They both stood, and Robert showed them out of the room.

"Nice to meet you, Serena. Thank you for speaking with us today."

"You're most welcome. I hope you can finally find Jackie's real killer. It would put our mind at rest now that she's been discovered."

"You have my word, we're going to do our very best for you both."

At the front door, Robert shook their hands. "You seem very capable detectives, and I'm sure you won't let us down. I know we lost Jackie years ago but I would still like to know what happened to her."

"We're determined to find out the truth."

"That's all we can ask. Goodbye."

Sally and Jack left the house. Robert closed the door gently behind them. They returned to the car, and Sally paused to look back at the house. Serena stared out of the window in their direction. Moments later, the woman peered over her shoulder and left the window.

"Nice couple."

"Hmm... maybe too nice," Jack replied.

They set off back to the station.

Once they'd left the grounds of the house, Sally asked her partner, "Right, what did you think of them?"

"I'm not getting a good vibe from them, that might just be me, though. Can't say it sits well with me that they're together now. The husband of a missing woman, presumed dead, who has now set up home with the woman's best friend. That's the pits, in my opinion."

"Wow, okay. I think we need to restrain our thoughts on that issue. If they were working together, searching for

Jackie, I suppose they were bound to become closer over time. Both grieving the loss of someone special."

"Yeah, if you put it that way." Jack shuddered. "Still doesn't gel with me. If anything happened to Donna and I moved her best friend into the house, I think Donna would come back and haunt me for the rest of my life."

Sally laughed. "Knowing your wife the way I do, yes, I can see why you'd think that. I don't know, they both seemed genuine enough to me. I didn't get the impression they were in cahoots to kill the wife off, but what do I know?"

"That's a little far-fetched even for you, boss. But yes, it's a plausible theory. He might have paid someone to have kidnapped her with the intention of killing her."

"Something we need to sink our teeth into. See if there were any large payments made from his bank account at the time of her disappearance."

"Or a few months before. Anyway, I'm glad they shed some light on how they could afford this place. Lucky buggers. What I wouldn't give to win the premium bonds."

Sally looked out of the corner of her eye at his reaction. "Have you got some money invested in them?"

"Er... no."

Sally creased up. "Then how are you expected to win anything?"

"I can dream. Hey, it would be nice to have a couple of quid in savings sitting in the bank. I haven't even got that under my belt, let alone any spare money to sink into investments."

"Back to the investigation. We'll spend the rest of the day going over the original file and formulating a plan."

"You mean making a list of where Falkirk screwed up and then making another list of who we need to interview over the next week or so."

Sally clicked her fingers. "Yes, that, too."

Jack groaned and settled lower into his seat and rested his head against the window. "Give me a dig in the ribs when we get back to base."

Sally left him to it and mulled over the conversation she'd just had with Serena and Robert while she drove.

CHAPTER 5

*L*orne and Jordan were getting ready to head out to the prison when Sally and Jack entered the office.

"How did it go?" Lorne asked.

"Are you two on your way out? It can wait until you get back."

"We've got a spare five minutes. I'm eager to know how your day has gone."

Sally sighed, removed her coat, perched on the desk opposite Lorne and draped her coat across her lap. "As well as to be expected, I suppose. We learnt something interesting today: the husband and the best friend are now married."

Lorne let out a low whistle. "Wow, really? Now that could lead to a motive for killing the wife off."

Sally stretched out her neck, to the left and then to the right. "We debated that in the car. We're going to check through the financial records of the husband, see what shows up."

"It might be worth checking the best friend's accounts, too, just in case she had the funds to pay a hitman to do the job."

Sally winked and raised a finger at Lorne. "Good call. Worth a punt for sure. Also, you should see the bloody mansion they're cozied up together in."

"It's like something out of *Dynasty*," Jack said, then added quickly, "Umm... not that I've ever watched the damn programme."

Sally and Lorne laughed.

"I didn't realise they were wealthy," Lorne said.

"They weren't, but they are now, courtesy of a win on the premium bonds. Out of this world, it is, universe even. I was nearly blinded by the bling in the chandelier at the bottom of the staircase. A-maz-ing, it was. And yes, my envy gene was on full alert," Sally replied dreamily.

"Wow! I take it you believe them?"

"I've got no grounds not to but, yes, we'll do the right thing and check into it tomorrow. Go, that's all we have so far. Will you be going home straight from the prison?"

"I hadn't planned to, but if you're giving us the go-ahead then Jordan and I can take both cars."

Jordan cringed. "I would, except I haven't got much fuel, sorry, I was going to fill up on the way home this evening. Would you mind dropping me back to the station, Lorne?"

She smiled. "Okay, as you've asked so nicely. We'd better get a wriggle on now."

"You do that. Give me a quick ring tonight to let me know how you got on, if you would?"

"I'll do that. Hopefully, we won't be home too late."

Sally nodded. "Good luck. Give him hell from me if he starts winding you up. Just be prepared for it."

"I will. I'm going to try and play him at his own game. We'll see you later."

· · ·

GOVERNOR WARD MET them in the reception area of HMP Norwich, after Lorne and Jordan had been searched. He shook their hands and smiled.

"Hello, Governor Ward, it's a pleasure to meet you. I want to thank you for allowing us to see Pickrel at such short notice."

"Always a pleasure to help the police out where I can. I'm not one of these governors who like to cause obstruction where other cases are concerned. I've arranged for Pickrel to see you in one of the interview rooms. I'll show you the way and leave you to it."

"Thank you, we appreciate your assistance in this matter. Hopefully, we'll be in and out within an hour."

Governor Ward raised his eyebrow and gestured for them to start walking. "Good luck with that one. You're aware how twisted he is, aren't you? In my opinion he likes nothing better than toying with the police. However, he might rethink how he treats you after what happened to him the other day."

Lorne paused and looked at him. "Sorry? What do you mean by that statement?"

"Only that he was beaten up by a few of the inmates. Now and again a situation gets fraught with tension. We do our best to clamp down on anything we see, nonetheless, in this instance, the attackers caught him in the showers, where we have limited guards monitoring the situation."

"I see. Was he badly hurt?"

"He spent the day in hospital as a precaution but was sent back to us after the doctor said they could do nothing further for him and the wounds would heal by themselves over the coming few weeks."

"What do you do in these circumstances? Keep him segregated?"

"We try. But it doesn't always work out that way. I don't

agree with keeping inmates locked up in solitary confinement twenty-four-seven, unlike some of my associates in my position. We each have our own way of working. I have an easy-going attitude, but when I'm pushed, the inmates see a different side of me."

"So he was thrown back into the lions' den, is that what you're telling us?"

"Not really. He's been confined to his cell. The problem is, he's a child killer, prisoners of that ilk don't tend to fare well behind bars, not nowadays. We do our best to keep each prisoner safe without mollycoddling them, but even we have our limits. We're understaffed the same way you are, I should imagine. We're stretched until the government gives us the go-ahead for another recruitment drive, which is imminent. The trouble is, the P word, the pandemic, has a lot to answer for as I'm sure you're aware. Crime rates are up since the lockdown was eased, and the number of staff is down. It's a no-win situation, and I can't see it getting any easier anytime soon."

"I agree, the country is in turmoil and appears to be getting worse every day."

He began walking again, and Lorne and Jordan followed suit.

"Still, there's very little point complaining, except to say that the government appears to be turning yet another blind eye at the overcrowding and underfunding of the prison system. There, I've voiced my opinion out loud, I can get off my soapbox now."

She smiled at him. "Sometimes we need to go through cathartic measures to put things right in our own heads."

"I'm with you there, Sergeant. How is DI Parker by the way? I was expecting her to show up here today as she was the one who arrested Pickrel, I believe. I do hope she isn't avoiding the place, what with her ex being imprisoned here."

"I don't think that's the case at all. Another high-priority investigation has come to our attention this week. I'm new to the team, I've come out of retirement to help Sally. I used to be an inspector down in London. Sally mentioned the Pickrel case to me and, let's just say it intrigued me that much I came out of retirement to help solve the remaining cases he could be connected to."

"Ah, yes. He hinted there might be another nine bodies out there, I seem to recall." He shook his head. "Nine children, do you think?"

"That's what we need to find out. We've got a file with a few missing persons we need to run past him. I need to gauge his reaction when I read out the names of the children."

"A word of warning: don't be fooled by him. Remember he escaped capture for over twenty years for his initial crime."

"I'm aware and will bear it in mind whilst we're interviewing him, I promise."

They walked on in silence until they reached the end of the long, narrow corridor.

He pushed the door open to the room on the right and stood back, allowing Jordan and Lorne to enter. "Make yourselves comfortable, he shouldn't be too long now. I'll gee up the guard bringing him."

"Thanks, we'll be fine here."

"I'll try and see you before you go if that's all right? I like to hear how these interviews pan out so I know what to expect from a prisoner and how he's likely to react over the next couple of days."

"We'll do that. See you soon."

He smiled and closed the door behind him.

Lorne and Jordan made themselves comfortable on the far side of the table.

"I wonder what state he's going to be in," Jordan said.

"We'll see soon enough. Serves him right. I never feel sorry when I hear a child killer or a paedophile gets hurt whilst doing time. In my opinion, that's the risk they take when they bloody commit their heinous crimes in the first place. If I had my way, they'd all have their dicks cut off and be transported to a desert island thousands of miles away, with only other dangerous criminals inhabiting the island. We wouldn't know if they killed each other or not, and I, for one, wouldn't frigging care."

Jordan sniggered, and he raised an eyebrow. "You're quite passionate about that suggestion, aren't you?"

"Too right I am. Sorry, now I'm riled up. I need to do some heavy breathing exercises to calm myself down before this little shit arrives. He's bound to have a detrimental effect on my emotions."

"Water off a duck's back to me. I treat them all the same. No matter what crimes they've committed, they're all fuckers who deserve what they get. If I hear one of them has either been beaten up or killed during their time inside, I shrug it off and generally think they deserved it."

"I think we all believe that at one time or another during our careers." For some reason Lorne's one and only true nemesis filtered into her mind. She shuddered and shook her arms out to calm herself down before Pickrel arrived.

"Are you okay? You appeared to drift off for a moment or two there."

She faced Jordan and nodded. "Yep, just revisited one of the worst criminals in history, who I had the pleasure of... how should I say this? Ah yes... killing off."

"Wow! You'll have to tell me the tale on the way back to the station."

She smiled at Jordan's eagerness. "Maybe. I've spent the past ten years trying to push the fucker aside, to prevent his image popping up in my mind, hampering my existence. See, he's still tormenting me from his grave."

"I understand that. Forget I asked. If in the future you feel like sharing, feel free, won't you?"

"You'll be the first to know."

Their conversation was interrupted by the door opening. A guard escorted the prisoner into the room. His hands were cuffed. He shuffled and sat at the table but avoided eye contact with Lorne and Jordan.

Lorne studied Pickrel through narrowed eyes. He had several bruises covering his face, one under each eye, and his nose was twisted to the right. Had it been broken during the assault? Lorne guessed that was probably the case.

"Hello, Louie. Thank you for agreeing to see us today."

Louie remained silent and stared at the wall over Lorne's shoulder.

"We're here to see if you wanted to add anything further to your statement about the other nine victims."

Again, his lips remained tightly closed.

Lorne stared at him. His hair was a tangled mess, his skin sallow and unhealthy-looking. He was truly a shadow of his former self, from what she'd seen in the photo of him she'd checked out before coming to see him. Saying that, she didn't feel sorry for him, not even a little bit. He deserved the thrashing he'd received, and any subsequent punishment he had coming his way in the future.

"You're making this very difficult, Louie, is that your intention?"

He shrugged and whispered, "Whatever, cop bitch."

The guard, who was waiting at the back of the room, stepped forward and shoved Pickrel in the back.

He turned on the guard. "Lay another hand on me, tosser, and I'll get you fired."

The guard retreated to his position and laughed. "In your dreams, shithead."

Ordinarily, Lorne would have reprimanded the guard for speaking in such a way to a prisoner, except this time, because of what Pickrel had been guilty of in the past, she had no intention of stepping in.

"Are you going to sit there and watch him abuse me like that?" Louie demanded.

"I didn't see anything out of the ordinary. You started it by calling me a derogatory name. It goes with the territory, I should imagine, right?"

"You're all the same. I'm sick of being treated like a lowlife around here."

"Really? By that I take it you're still in denial about killing your sister, is that right?"

"Nope. I killed her all right. I admitted that much."

"Then I don't understand why you should complain about the way you're being treated."

"Are you for real? I have rights, human rights that these guys need to adhere to."

"You have a bed to sleep on and food in your belly, don't you?"

"Of course I do. Edible food is debatable at times. And don't think I don't see the spittle floating on my dinner most days."

She cringed at the thought but again refused to feel sorry for him. "Oh well. You'll need to take that up with the governor, there's nothing I can do about it."

"Yeah, right, as if he's likely to listen to my complaints."

"Yeah, that's all they are, complaints, you never bloody stop," added the guard.

Lorne had to suppress a giggle. "What if I put a deal on the table?"

Pickrel's gaze latched on to hers. He inclined his head and asked, "What type of deal and for what?"

Lorne tapped her finger on the file she had in front of her. "How about you tell me where some of your victims are buried and I'll have a word with the governor for you? See if I can't ease things for you a little around here?" She looked over at the guard, who was shaking his head in disgust, then back to Pickrel, who appeared to be mulling the proposition over.

He kept quiet for a while and then he stared at Lorne, long and hard. "Show me what you have in the file."

Lorne smiled. "Not until you agree to help us."

He laughed. "I'll scratch your back and you scratch mine compromise, that's what you're asking, isn't it?"

She shrugged. "If that's what you want to call it. I was under no misapprehension that our coming here today would just be a formality."

"Good. I'm glad I didn't let you down."

"Ah, but you are. Before I show you the photos, you have to agree to help us."

"Or else?" he challenged, his eyes blazing as they seared into hers.

"You live your life in fear behind bars. Either way, it doesn't matter to me." Lorne was hoping her double bluff would work. She could see him working through the options in his mind.

Suddenly, his face lit up. Which made her a tad suspicious about what he was going to either say or do next. Jordan nudged his knee against hers under the table. She resisted the temptation to turn his way and nudged him back.

"Okay, let's see the file. But you have to call the wolves off, I have certain requests I need to action first."

"Okay, let's hear them."

"I want to be put in solitary, for my own protection, the

governor has failed to do that so far. To me, that's neglecting his duties. I want that changed. I'd rather sit in a cell away from the others for the rest of my life than walk amongst them not knowing if I'll get jumped on or not."

"You have my word, I'll see what I can do."

He sat back and folded his arms. "I'll wait here until you get that agreed."

Lorne glanced up to see the guard shaking his head again.

"I doubt if the boss will agree to his demands," the guard said. "We don't negotiate with the prisoners."

"Not even if he's willing to help us identify other victims?"

"Not even that."

Lorne pushed back her chair and took the file with her. "I won't be long," she told Jordan. She noticed the amusement in Pickrel's eyes as she flew past him.

"Hey, you can't go walking around this prison unaccompanied, as if you own the place," the guard shouted.

Lorne stood with her hand on the doorknob. "Then get someone to accompany me to the governor's office."

He huffed out a breath and got on his radio. After requesting backup, he hissed, "Someone will be here in a jiffy. You'll have to wait until they get here."

"Good, I'll wait outside." She left the room.

A couple of minutes later, another guard came to collect her. He greeted her with a stern expression, and she found herself shrivelling under his glare.

"Come this way."

"Thanks, I'm sorry to put you out like this. It's important—"

He raised a hand to stop her. "I couldn't give a toss. Save your excuses for the governor."

Bugger! That told me. The last thing I wanted to do was tick the

111

staff off. I hope the governor will at least listen to what I have to say.

The guard rapped on the door and waited for Governor Ward to invite them in.

He bellowed for them to enter. Instead of being confronted by the mild-mannered, amenable man who had shown them into the interview room barely ten minutes before, Lorne faced an extremely vexed man. "Sergeant, what's the meaning of this?"

"I'm sorry. I didn't mean to step on anyone's toes, especially not yours, Governor Ward. You're aware how imperative it is that we speak to Pickrel about the victims, and he said he's not willing to do that until he gets 'special treatment'."

"It's not going to happen, Sergeant. We have a rule in place not to pander to the prisoners. Can you imagine the uproar there will be if word got out that I gave him special treatment? We'd have a full-scale riot on our hands within minutes."

"I didn't think of that," Lorne admitted, her head dipping in shame.

"Then you need to pack up and leave."

Her head shot up, and she pleaded, "No, sorry, let me give it another try. I'll work around his request, or try to."

"You've got half an hour to do just that or you will be escorted from the premises."

"I understand. Please accept my apologies."

He waved the suggestion away, dismissing the notion and her, as he got back to his work.

The guard led the way back down the long hallway. Lorne gulped several times en route, trying her hardest to compose herself by the time she entered the room.

She retook her seat and smiled at Pickrel. "I've just run it past the governor, and he's in agreement, only if you give us the locations of where the victims we have with us today are buried."

Pickrel applauded her. "Well done, Sergeant. I didn't think you would have it in you to pull it off."

Her cheeks flushed. She wasn't in the habit of lying, but she had an urgent need to gather the information for the sake of the families involved. "Shall we begin?"

"Let me see the file." Pickrel held out his hand and wiggled his fingers.

"No, I'll show you the photos one by one and you can tell me their names."

"That's assuming I know their names."

"You will. Their names would have been circulated by the media at the time of their disappearance, so don't try that one on me."

He had the audacity to wink at her, and it made her skin crawl with uncertainty whether she was going to be able to pull this precarious scheme of hers off or not. "All right, let's see what you have for me."

Lorne took one of the photos from the file and slid it towards him. He picked up the Polaroid snap and traced his finger around the young girl's face, making Lorne want to vomit. "Ah yes, this young thing was one of my first kills, not long after I got on the road as a salesman. Feisty, catty wench. She fought me every step of the way."

"Where did you pick her up?" Lorne looked at the notes in the file regarding the girl's disappearance to see if his account matched.

He tipped his head back and studied the ceiling as he thought. "Ah, yes, it's all coming back to me now. All the delicious details, in glorious colour." He ran his tongue across his swollen lips.

Bile rose in her throat, but she was determined not to let her true feelings show. "Get on with it."

His gaze dropped to her once more. "She was walking home from school. That's the trouble with folks in the country, have you noticed how many people let their kids walk home by themselves? It was irresponsible of her parents. Parents are the pits, those who don't give a shit about their kids. I dished out my punishment on the kids, knowing that the parents would suffer for the rest of their lives. Or would they? Have you revisited them yet? To see if they're still riddled with guilt? Even though I picked Tina up first," he tapped the photo he had placed back on the table, then continued, "the other parents did nothing to keep their children safe. What was the matter with them? It was as though they were deliberately ignoring the news bulletins, the warnings through the media to keep their kids safe. They did nothing. On my travels up and down that road, I saw kid after kid walking alone, even when the clocks went back and the evenings grew darker. None of them deserved to be parents."

"In your opinion. So, killing the children meant nothing, is that what you're telling us? It was all about you dishing out the punishment to the adults, the parents."

He smiled and winced as his busted-up lips stretched apart. "Oh, I wouldn't necessarily say that. I enjoyed the thrill of the capture and watching them take their last breath." He let out a demonic laugh.

Lorne clenched her fists. He stared at her hands and laughed again.

"Tempted to lash out, aren't you, Sergeant? Go on, make my day."

Lorne shook her head. "It's not going to happen." She took back the photo and removed another one from the folder and pushed it towards him. "What about this little girl, do you remember her name and the circumstances in which you picked her up?"

"Of course I do. This one was Alison Frost. I followed her and her friend down the main road; they didn't have a clue I was behind them. Her friend stopped off at one of the farms along the route, and that left Alison, on foot, with the night drawing in. I stopped to give her a lift, told her that her mother had sent me because she was worried about her, and bingo-bango, the job was a good 'un and she was one of my easier kills. Happened in the back of my car."

Lorne nodded and swapped the photos with a new one, another girl.

"Ah yes, Lucy. Now then, how did I kill her? That's right, I grabbed her as she walked through the woods. Fancy a girl of that age taking a shortcut home through woodland. Again, the parents are at fault. Do you have children, Sergeant?"

"I'm not here to discuss myself or my family," she replied curtly.

"Ah, you're being very defensive, I'm guessing you do. Would you allow them to walk the streets alone, inviting someone to abduct them?"

Seething, Lorne cleared her throat. Without replying, she swapped the photos again and slid the only image of a boy victim in front of Pickrel. "And this one, what about him?"

Pickrel held her gaze for a while and then studied the photo. "Timothy. He was worse than the females. Squealed, kicked and hissed like a girl when I grabbed him off his bike. He was on his paper round, far too young to be working at that age, if you ask me."

"All right, now you've named them all and admitted you killed them, why don't you tell us where their bodies are buried?"

"Why should I?" He clenched his hands together and sighed.

"To give the families closure."

He tilted his head and narrowed his eyes. "You mean the same families who let them down in the first place?"

"If that's what you truly believe, yes."

His eyes widened, as if an important thought had popped into his mind. "How are my wife and daughter getting along? Have you seen them?"

"I have no idea, and no, I haven't seen them."

He fell silent and grinned. "I'll tell you where the bodies are buried, but only if Natalie brings Crystal to see me."

CHAPTER 6

"He said what?" Sally shouted the second Lorne revealed what Pickrel's demands were. "What an absolute fucking shit, he is. Not only has he robbed those poor families of their children and is refusing to tell us where they're buried, but he's determined to destroy what little happiness Natalie has probably found since he was banged up. We can't put her through this, we just can't."

They were having the discussion in Sally's office over a cup of coffee. Lorne reclined in her chair and took a sip from her drink. Weary and emotionally wrought after confronting Pickrel at the prison, she sighed heavily. "He's the scum of the earth, there's no other way to describe the fucker. All the way through the conversation I had to resist the urge to scratch myself, he definitely made my skin bloody crawl. Such a smarmy shit."

Sally took her hand off her cup and ran her fingers through her hair. "We're at an impasse. He's revelling in the fact that he's got us by the short and curlies."

"Yep, I thought the same. We're damned if we do and

damned if we don't. What a frigging nightmare situation to find ourselves in. What do you suggest I do next?"

After wetting her dry mouth with coffee, Sally shrugged. "You're going to have to bow to his demands." She raised a hand when Lorne opened her mouth to fling an objection her way. "Hear me out. All you can do is lay it on the line with Natalie. I think she trusts us. She'll appreciate that we wouldn't want to put her through such a traumatic position if there was a way around it. When I had to go to see her, to explain why we had arrested her husband, she broke down, sobbed continually for a good ten minutes before she came up for air. I asked her if she had any inclination that he was a serial killer. She broke down again, as though I was accusing her of harbouring a criminal. I wasn't, not in the slightest, nevertheless, I had to know if he'd even hinted at anything over the years. You know what some killers are like, some of them get a buzz out of speaking about what might be a hypo-thetical case when what they're really talking about is some-thing they've been at the centre of over the years."

"What a dreadful position to find herself in, I feel for her. What do you think I should do, go and see her? Call her and discuss it over the phone?"

"No, don't do the latter. Put it this way, if that was my husband, I'd want to hear about something like this first-hand and in person. Why don't we call it a night? Go home, jump in the bath, have a nice soak to get the grime of being in the same room as that arsehole off of you and ring her in the morning, first thing."

Lorne downed the rest of her drink. "Are you going to tell me how you got on today?"

"Nope. I'm shattered. Desperate to get out of here. I need to get home, I'm sure you feel the same way after the day you've had."

"Totally. I'm going to head home then."

"You go ahead, I'll switch everything off and see you in the morning. Try not to dwell on things."

Lorne smirked. "You know me so well. See you in the morning, Sal."

DURING THE DRIVE HOME, Lorne replayed the interview with Pickrel over and over in her mind. Not concentrating where she was going, she found herself doing a U-turn in the middle of the road once she'd realised she'd overshot the lane that led to her house.

The dogs were making a racket when she got out of the car. Tony greeted her on the doorstep.

"Everything all right? Why are they kicking off?"

He offered up a weak smile and hooked an arm around her shoulder once she'd joined him. He kissed her gently on the forehead. "You'll see."

She glanced up at him. "Tony? You're worrying me."

He refused to say anything else and guided her through the house and out to the kennels.

"Can't I at least get changed first?"

"You can do that in a minute. I need to show you some-thing first."

"Sounds mysterious. What is it?"

"You'll find out soon enough."

She picked up on the tension in his tone that she hadn't recognised when he'd greeted her. She surveyed the yard, searching for anything new or out of place, and then she spotted it. The wheelbarrow across the other side of the courtyard, close to the kennel run. "Oh no. Don't tell me we've lost one of our babies."

"Sorry, love. I debated whether to bury her before you got home but realised how foolish that would be, not allowing you to say goodbye."

She cocked her head up towards him, and he kissed her on the lips. "You're a thoughtful man. Who is it?"

"Taliah. She was getting on when she came to us, we were aware of that, love."

"I know. It doesn't make it any easier, knowing that she spent the last days of her life in a concrete kennel. Had I known she was on her last legs I would have insisted she end her days in the house, with us."

"They can't tell us if something is wrong. She had a good life with us, better than if she'd been at a different rescue centre. At least our kennels have comfortable beds, lots of blankets and heating on in the winter."

"I know. What happened?"

"It was during the exercise slot. I had taken the dogs on either side of her, and at first, she just sat there, in her basket at the back, not budging an inch. I went in there, tried to coax her out of her bed. Eventually she stood up but collapsed right away. She looked up at me, and I saw it in her eyes. She was pleading with me to let her go. I picked her up and put her back in her bed. She placed her paw on my hand, as if thanking me for my kindness, closed her eyes and took her last breath."

Lorne wiped away the tears and swallowed down the large lump blocking her throat. She touched a hand to Tony's cheek. "You're a kind and caring soul, Tony Warner. I'm glad you were there with her at the end."

"Do you want me to bury her tonight or shall I leave her in the shed and bury her tomorrow?"

"Let's leave it for tonight. I heard on the radio in the car that it's supposed to be a sunny day tomorrow. Wish I could be here, but we're snowed under at work, so the onus lies on your shoulders again, sorry, love."

"Don't be. You're busy, I know that. Want to say your goodbyes alone?"

Lorne smiled and nodded. "I won't be long."

"I'll stick the kettle on. Take your time."

Lorne crossed the courtyard, and the din from the other dogs ceased. *They know. I'm their pack leader, they know that Taliah is gone and that I'll be grieving for her.* Lorne bent down and stroked the dog that had come to them the year before when her elderly owner had passed away from cancer. "I'm sorry I let you down, baby. Had I known that you were ill, I would have ensured your final days were with us, comfortable inside the house. Forgive me. Run free, little girl. You're probably up there now, reunited with old Cyril, I know how much you missed him. Maybe you were too brokenhearted when he left us to want to carry on. I shall miss your kisses and the way you always placed a paw on my shoulder, as if thanking me for taking good care of you. In the end, it wasn't enough, was it? Be happy, come back and visit us one day. Make a sign, let us know you're there."

Tony called out her name from the back door. She waved and gave him the thumbs-up and then bent to kiss Taliah on the tip of her nose. "Know that you were loved, little one."

She wiped away the tears as they appeared, covered Taliah with an old coat she found in the store room, wheeled her into a shed in case the weather changed and returned to the house.

Tony deposited the two mugs of coffee on the kitchen table and sat down. He pulled out the chair next to him and gestured for Lorne to join him. "Are you all right?"

"I'll be fine. It's such a shame when we lose a member of our family, after all, that's what they are. Come here, Sheba." Her faithful GSD crossed the room to sit in front of her and rested her chin on Lorne's knee. "Even she knows something is up. Hey, cheer up, sweetie. We'll give Taliah a compassionate farewell. Won't we, Tony? When I say we, I mean you."

He smiled. "Leave it to me. I won't let her down, you know that. Did you have a good day at work?"

"Nope. Next question."

"Bugger. I take it you don't want to talk about it then?"

"You guessed right. I'll have this and jump in the bath if that's okay?"

"Sure. I'll go out and feed the hounds in a moment. I made a curry earlier, so dinner is all sorted for later."

"What would I do without you?"

He shrugged. "Starve, sometimes."

Lorne reached over and gathered his hand in hers until Sheba moaned and she slipped one hand back to stroke her. "How's your day been, apart from the obvious?"

"The same as usual. I've made a start clearing out the shed at the far end. I want to make it watertight so it gives us extra storage for blankets and beds et cetera."

"What an excellent idea. Once it's finished, I can run another ad in the local paper, asking for donations of quilts and blankets and whatnot. We received a good response from the locals the last time I ran one."

"I remember we were inundated with old quilts, most of which we've used now. It shouldn't take me long." He rubbed the top of his leg. "Providing this doesn't start playing up again."

"You need to see the doctor. I feel guilty for putting you under extra strain running this place on your own."

"It is what it is, love. We can't afford to employ anyone else. It'll be fine, once I get into a routine."

"Let me know if it all gets too much for you, especially if your leg is giving you gyp. I realise now how selfish I have been. Getting this place and then ditching it, leaving it all to you while I go back to work."

He tipped his head back and laughed. "Hardly selfish. You're bringing in a wage again, that's the main consideration. I can deal with the dogs. Just promise me you won't take on any more."

"I promise. Mind if I jump in the bath now? I can feed the dogs if you want me to."

"Go, I'll be fine. Don't rush either, have a long soak. I'll put the water back on, make sure we have enough for the washing up later."

She smiled, stood, kissed him and left the room. After removing her coat and shoes at the front door, she flew up the stairs and ran the water, pouring in a good measure of lavender bubble bath at the same time. Then she dived into the bedroom, stripped off and slipped on her towelling robe. Returning to the bathroom, she sat on the toilet and scrolled through her phone until her bath was ready. She saw that her sister, Jade, had tried to call her a couple of times. She'd forgotten to take her phone off silent after she'd finished seeing Pickrel. Bracing herself for an ear-battering, she rang Jade.

"Hi, how are you?"

"Only just returning my call after four hours? Are you kidding me, Lorne? What if it was a dire emergency?"

Lorne slipped off her robe and sank into the bath. "Was it?"

"No, not this time, but it could have been, and you'd be none the wiser."

"I'm sorry, Jade. You know I started back to work this week. I'm up to my neck in an important case right now. I don't have time during the day to accept personal calls."

"Four bloody hours!" Jade shouted, unnecessarily repeating herself.

"I heard you the first time. Are you going to turn this into a slanging match? If that's your intention, I'm going to hang up now. I've had the worst day imaginable at work and came home to find one of my dogs had died. So, if you wouldn't mind reining in your temper a little..."

"I'm sorry. It was thoughtless of me to go on the attack. I should have realised you were back at work. It always was the be all and end all to you, wasn't it?"

Lorne groaned inwardly and puffed out her cheeks. "Give it a rest, Jade. Don't start something you'll regret."

"Jesus, have you heard yourself? Dishing out threats like that. Who the hell do you think you are?"

Lorne growled and pressed the End Call button and switched her phone off. She'd had her share of Jade's dramas over the years to last her a bloody lifetime. No more. I have no intention of taking any further shit from her. Not today, not tomorrow, not ever. If that means we fall out, never to be reunited, then so be it. At least my life will be a darn sight quieter from now on.

Jade had succeeded in riling her up. So much for having a relaxing bath to ease away the stresses of the day. Taking a few deep breaths, she did her best to calm the blood tearing through her veins.

Thirty minutes later, Tony appeared in the doorway. "Are you still with us? I thought you might have dropped off."

"No. I've been contemplating summoning up enough energy to get out."

"No rush. The dogs are all fed now. I thought I'd come up, see what you fancy with your curry, rice or pasta?"

"I think rice, that is, if that's what you want?"

"I'm easy. How long are you going to be? My stomach has been rumbling so much, I almost started on the dog food while I was feeding them."

"Crikey, all right, I'm getting out now."

"Have another ten minutes, the rice will take between twenty minutes and half an hour anyway."

"Thanks. I'll be down shortly."

· · ·

AFTER THEY'D EATEN and discussed where to bury Taliah, they took the rest of the bottle of wine into the lounge. Snuggled up on the sofa, she told him about the call she'd made to Jade.

"Did you find out what was wrong in the end?"

Lorne sighed. "Nope. She was too busy having a bloody go at me to tell me. I refuse to ring her back, I'm quite within my rights after the way she spoke to me."

"Give her a break. We both have to accept she's a drama queen. On the other hand, if she was reaching out and got narky with you for not calling her back, maybe, just maybe, there's something more to her trying to get hold of you than you realise."

She took a sip of her wine. "You're right. Here goes, let me try and ring her now. I'll put it on speakerphone, and you can hear how she speaks to me."

Lorne turned on the phone to find several missed calls and a couple of voicemail messages from her sister. "Shit. I'm going to need to prepare myself for a backlash now."

"Maybe you should listen to the voicemails first before you call her."

She did. The first one was Jade talking gibberish; somewhere thrown into the mix she heard a mumbled apology from her sister.

"That's a good sign." Tony smiled.

"We'll soon see. Here goes." She rang Jade's designated number in her phone. It rang a couple of times, and then her sister's weary voice answered.

"I wanted some advice from you."

"What type of advice, legal?"

"Possibly," Jade replied.

"Do you want to give me a hint?" Although Jade fell silent, her heavy breathing increased, prompting Lorne to ask, "Jade, what in God's name is going on?"

Another few seconds' hesitation, and then her sister revealed the truth. "I got caught, shoplifting."

Lorne sat upright on the edge of the sofa and stared at Tony. "You what?"

"You heard me. I don't know how or what happened. One minute I was walking around the clothes shop in town and the next I went to walk out of the shop and was accosted by the security guard who came from nowhere."

"And what did you take?"

"That's just it, I don't remember taking anything. I've never been in this situation before, I'm as honest as an eighty-year-old nun, for God's sake."

"So how did the item get in your bag or wherever it was?"

"The dress ended up in my shopping bag. I didn't even like the dress. I reckon someone planted it on me."

"Never. Why would they do that?"

Jade burst into tears. "I don't know... I was hoping you could tell me."

"How would I know? Damn, Jade, don't get upset. That's not going to help the issue, is it?"

"What is?"

"We'll sort something out. Were you taken to the police station?"

"No, thank God. The shop let me off with a warning."

"Then what's the problem? You said you needed advice, what about?"

"I want to sue the bloody shop for accusing me of something I didn't do."

"But the goods were found on you."

"I know that."

"Then you don't have a leg to stand on. If they've let you off with a warning, my advice would be to forget about it, Jade."

"A big help you've turned out to be. Sorry to have laid all this on your doorstep."

"What? Why have a pop at me? What can I do about it?"

"Show some compassion for a start. Goodnight, Lorne."

With that, Jade ended the call.

Lorne threw the phone on the end of the sofa and shook her head. "I give up. I was never going to win that one, was I?"

"Sorry, but no, you weren't. She'll soon calm down. Give her time."

"I'm done with her, Tony. Fed up with her always having a go at me for no damn reason. She needs to grow up, once and for all."

He rubbed her shoulders, relieving the tension which had developed since getting out of the bath and speaking to her sister. "Better?"

She turned to kiss him. "Your healing hands always make things right."

They spent the rest of the evening cuddled up on the couch. Lorne felt guilty about not visiting the dogs and bedding them down for the night, but Tony insisted he would carry out the nightly routine to give her a break.

As soon as her head hit the pillow, she fell asleep, only to wake up at two in the morning, the Pickrel case and the impossible dilemma ahead of her prominent in her mind.

CHAPTER 7

*L*orne and Jordan arrived at Natalie's house at around nine forty-five the next morning. Lorne wrung her hands anxiously while they waited for Natalie to answer the door.

Instead, the door was answered by a man in his late fifties-early sixties with a greying beard and a stern expression. "You must be the police. Natalie rang me, asked me to be here with her. I take it you have no objections."

Lorne smiled and produced her warrant card. "DS Lorne Warner, and my partner, DC Jordan Reid, sir."

"I'm Jeremy Hines, pleased to meet you. Come in, out of this vile weather. Non-stop rain at the moment, I think we're all fed up with it by now."

He stood back, allowing them access to the hallway.

"Thanks. More floods predicted, so they've just announced on the radio on the way over here," Lorne replied.

"Not good. Come through, Natalie has just fed the baby. I've finally persuaded her to move in with us for a bit, while she sells this place. She hates being here alone, after sharing it with that bastard."

Lorne nodded, totally understanding his daughter's point of view. He led the way into the lounge. Natalie was on the sofa, rocking the baby in her arms. Lorne and Jordan sat on another sofa opposite.

"Hello, Natalie. I can't thank you enough for seeing us at such short notice."

"Anything I can do to help keep that man in prison and away from my daughter is fine by me. Take a seat. She's going to sleep now, I'll just put her down for a little while. I won't be a moment." Natalie went to stand, but her father rushed forward. "Oh no you don't, you leave her to me."

"Thanks, Dad. You're a treasure."

He took the baby and left the room. Natalie fidgeted in her seat under Lorne's gaze.

"How have you been, since the birth?" Lorne asked.

Natalie's gaze was drawn to a photo on the mantelpiece of her father with a woman whom Lorne presumed was her mother. "Without my parents' support, I would have been lost. They've been amazing. Mum is out most mornings, she's a care assistant, and it's Dad's day off today. He insisted on being here, I hope that's all right?"

"Of course, it is. Would you rather wait until he comes back?"

"If you don't mind. Can I get you a drink? Tea or coffee?"

"We wouldn't want to put you out."

"You're not. What would you like?" Her voice was fraught with emotion.

"Two coffees would be perfect, thank you."

"I'll be right back." She darted out of her seat and closed the door behind her.

"She seems nervous," Jordan commented.

"She does. I suppose it's to be expected in the circumstances."

"I wonder what her reaction is going to be like."

"I think it'll be her father's reaction we'll need to be wary of."

Jordan crossed his arms and sat back on the sofa. "Oh great! I'll look forward to that one and brace myself for him kicking off."

Lorne chuckled. "Just follow my lead and you'll be fine." She surveyed the room and noticed that all the soft furnishings matched in a discrete way; someone had a designer's eye in the family. Lorne had been partial to interior design and renovating houses, back in the day, before she had turned to saving desperate and unloved dogs in her spare time. She suspected Natalie had a subtle keen eye for colour.

"She's all settled now." Natalie's father entered the room. "Where's Natalie?"

"Making a drink," Lorne replied.

"I'll be right back."

A few seconds later, Natalie entered the room carrying a tray with four mugs and a sugar bowl on it. "I forgot to ask if you take sugar, sorry, I've already put the milk in."

"Thanks for going to so much trouble." Lorne smiled. "We have one sugar each."

After Natalie sugared the drinks, her father distributed the mugs then sat on the arm of the easy chair, next to his daughter.

"Why are you here?" Natalie asked. "I thought once he'd been arrested and put in prison that would be the end of it and yet, here you are, paying me another visit. Why?"

Lorne wrapped her hands around the mug, and her gaze met Natalie's. "This might be an uncomfortable meeting. I'll try to explain things the best I can, but it's not going to be easy for you to hear. Please bear with me."

Natalie glanced up at her father.

He flung an arm around her shoulders. "It'll be all right, love. Go on, Sergeant."

Butterflies took flight in Lorne's stomach. "Do you remember when your husband—?"

Her father grunted. "Er... you can stop calling him that, she's divorcing him."

"Sorry, I wasn't aware of that. Okay, when Louie was originally arrested and questioned, he hinted that there might be more bodies out there."

"We're aware of what was said at the time," Natalie's father said abruptly.

"Well, as part of a Cold Case Unit, we couldn't let things lie there. Just like Mrs Pickrel wanted closure for the death of her child, we believe the parents of Louie's other victims deserve the same opportunity to bid farewell to their loved ones."

"Jesus! What are you saying?" Natalie's father demanded, his face flushing with anger.

Cautiously, Lorne continued, "Well, Jordan and I visited Louie yesterday in the hope that he would reveal who his victims were and how he disposed of their bodies. We were under the impression there were nine further victims. We've trawled through old cold cases and missing person files and come up with four likely victims. We showed Louie the pictures of the victims, and there was instant recognition in his eyes."

"Good, at least he has the decency to admit his sins now," Mr Hines huffed out his response.

"Dad, please, let her finish. What are you trying to say, Sergeant?" Natalie asked.

"We're desperate to give the parents of the victims the news they've waited years to hear but we need your help, Natalie."

"What? How?" Natalie asked.

"Yes, do enlighten us, Sergeant," her father said sarcastically.

Lorne sipped at her drink, contemplating how she should proceed. "I'm just going to come out and tell you what he said. He told us he's willing to divulge where the bodies are if you take baby Crystal to see him in the prison."

Natalie's mouth dropped open, and she stared at Lorne while her father leapt to his feet and paced the room. He ran his hands through his short, grey hair.

"You have got to be out of your mind, lady. There is no way my daughter will agree to bow down to his disgusting blackmail. Yes, that's what this amounts to, *blackmail.*"

"I'm sorry. I appreciate how utterly disgusting this must be to hear, but if you could just find it in your heart to think about the other families and the torment they must still be going through after all these years," Lorne pleaded, emotion tipping her voice up another level.

"I won't allow it. You have no right coming here, putting my daughter in this untenable position. I'll be speaking to your superior about this. Now get out of this house."

Natalie jumped to her feet and grabbed her father's flailing arms. "Dad, you're going to have to calm down. You know what the doctor said, you're not to get excited or angry."

"Is there something wrong, sir, are you ill?" Lorne asked.

"He's got heart problems. The doctor told him he needs to take early retirement, but he's refusing to do it, which is driving me and Mum potty. Please stop pacing and sit down, Dad."

"Your daughter is right, sir. There's no point getting yourself worked up like this," Lorne chipped in.

Natalie managed to coerce her father to take a seat again and held on tightly to his hands.

"How can you come here and ask the impossible and not expect us to get uptight?" Mr Hines shook his head in disbelief.

"I wouldn't, not ordinarily. It's only because of the loved ones left behind, sir. The last thing I wanted to do was come here today to add extra pressure on your daughter's shoulders."

Natalie's head dropped, and she stared at the electric fire for what seemed like an age. "I'll do it."

"What?" Her father bounced up onto his feet again.

Natalie clawed at him, searching for his hands, and pulled him back down beside her. "Dad, listen. This isn't about what we want, or what he wants, for that matter, I'll be doing it for the families. They have a right to know where their children are buried. Put yourself in their shoes and stop being so selfish."

"Selfish? Is that what you think of me, even though I'm prepared to open my house to you and that bastard's child?"

Natalie gasped. "Dad, how could you? This isn't Crystal's fault. She didn't ask to be spawned by a serial killer." Natalie's tough exterior crumbled. "Oh God, you forced me to say it. I've been trying to not revisit that ghastly thought since the day I found out what he was guilty of."

Her father wrapped his arms around Natalie. "I'm sorry. I should never have called him that, darling."

Lorne watched the interaction between the father and daughter, and it reminded her of her relationship with her own father. He had loved her fiercely, none more so than when he'd tried to help get her daughter, Charlie, back from the vile Unicorn. Lorne's own father had been abducted and traumatised by two of the villain's goons around the same time. She never wanted to revisit that encounter again, not anytime soon.

"Dad, I have to do this. Please understand, I don't want to

fall out with you about my decision. I'm not a selfish person, if I can help these people achieve the justice they deserve for their loved ones, then so be it."

Lorne raised a finger. "If it helps, maybe you should put a different spin on things to make it more palatable."

"What are you talking about?" her father asked, his features distorted with a mixture of confusion and anger.

"Consider this: if we can pin the other murders on him, he will be tried for each additional murder, therefore, the likelihood of him getting out of prison will disappear overnight."

Her father nodded as he contemplated Lorne's statement. "I get that. I don't like it, but it's definitely worth considering now."

Natalie smiled and touched her father's cheek with the palm of her hand. "I knew you'd see sense eventually. How many times do we hear about prisoners getting let out on a technicality? I live with the thought of him being released daily, Dad. It's hard to deal with, some days more than others. I have to help the police, if only to retain my sanity."

Her father gathered her in his arms again and sighed. "I love you so much. I live with the guilt of not seeing through that bastard in the first place. I should have realised something was wrong with him, I didn't."

"Neither of us did, Dad. How do you think I feel? Being duped by him. Jesus, even his own mother was deceived by him for years. He's a manipulative deviant, there's no other word for it. Let's do all we can to knock him down a peg or two. He'll be rubbing his hands at the chance of seeing me and his child, but we'll have the upper hand at all times. Maybe his focus is too much on us and he hasn't even considered the consequences."

Lorne nodded. "I believe Natalie is correct."

Her father growled, and his shoulders slumped in defeat.

"All right, I hear you. If you believe you can handle seeing him again, then I won't object or stand in your way."

Natalie smiled and kissed her father on the cheek. "Thank you for having faith in me after all I've put you through over this past year."

He placed his hands on either side of her face. "You haven't let me down, you could never do that, Nat." He turned to face Lorne and asked, "Where do we go from here? And yes, I'll agree to my daughter going to the prison on one proviso."

Natalie rolled her eyes up to the ceiling. "Dad!"

"Go on," Lorne replied. "What proviso?"

Her father pointed at Lorne. "You go with her and he remains in handcuffs during the visit."

Lorne nodded. "That goes without saying. I'll be there, we'll both be there with your daughter every step of the way, I promise."

"When will this visit take place?" Mr Hines asked.

"Whenever suits your daughter, it's not like he's going anywhere. Oops… I might need to warn you about something before you lay eyes on him again."

"What's that?" Natalie asked.

"I'm afraid he's not looking his best at the moment."

Her father laughed loudly. "He's been beaten up, hasn't he?"

Lorne smirked. "I believe it's called karma, sometimes she can be a copper's best ally."

Natalie and her father laughed, but she still seemed shocked by the news.

"Right, thank you for the coffee," Lorne said. "I'll be in touch when we've made the arrangements. Is there any day you can't manage in the next week or so?"

"I have no appointments booked for Crystal, so any day is fine by me. How will I get there?"

"We'll come and pick you up, that's not a problem."

"Thank you."

"I'll be in touch soon. Try not to worry about the visit, we won't let anything happen to either you or Crystal. I'll ensure two guards are present, if necessary."

"That'll put my mind at ease."

Her father showed them to the door and pointed at Lorne. "If anything goes wrong and she gets hurt, I'll come after you, Sergeant."

"It won't. Have faith in us, sir."

He nodded and closed the door behind them.

"That was a tough ask, for them both," Jordan said on the way back to the car.

"It was. Not a lot of people have the faith they once had in the police, not after recent events which have played out in the media. They have every right to feel concerned. But they also have the A-team on their side, and we won't let them down, will we?"

"No intention of doing that, Lorne, no way. When are you looking at going?"

"My idea was to try and make the appointment ASAP, just in case whoever knocked seven bells out of him tries to finish off the job in the next few days."

"Do you think that's likely?"

Lorne got in the car, and Jordan joined her. They buckled up. "I suppose there's every possibility if they've struck once."

They drove back to the station and found Sally and Jack standing by the door to the office.

"Ah, you're back. We're just heading off. How did it go with Natalie?" Sally asked.

"Her father wasn't too enamoured with the suggestion, but Natalie managed to talk him around, eventually."

"Good news. When are you planning on going to the prison?"

"I'm going to give the governor a call now, unless you want us to get on with anything else in your absence."

"I don't. The rest of the team are working on the information we've gathered so far, which isn't much. You continue with your case. Go through the files a couple more times in case any other victims catch your eye. Maybe broaden the criteria you were searching for."

"We'll do that. Good luck with your quest."

"Thanks, we're going to need it. We have a long list of people we need to interview."

Lorne and Jordan sat at their respective desks. She rang the prison and spoke to the governor. He gave them the go-ahead to come anytime during the next week or so. Lorne was eager to get the meeting organised ASAP so opted for that afternoon at two. With that tied up with the governor, she rang Natalie with the details.

"Thank you. Not long to wait. What time will you pick me up?"

"Around one-fifteen, if that suits you? Just in case the traffic is bad in Norwich, you never know."

"Yes, it was a nightmare the last time I visited, that was a couple of months ago. I'll see you later."

Lorne ended the call and then helped Jordan to search through the files again for the umpteenth time. "We'll know these off by heart soon enough," she quipped.

"You're not wrong."

Sally and Jack worked through the list, deciding to go through it in alphabetical order. Some of the partygoers that night had moved house and were trickier to find than others. But locate them, they did, eventually. Only for them to be told the same thing over and over. All of their accounts of what had happened at the party that night matched what Robert and Serena had told them.

Here they were at the final location, that of Serena's ex-husband, Denis. He opened the door to the flat in Wymondham town centre. He seemed dishevelled, had two or three days' stubble and swayed a lot in the doorway as he tried to focus on who was standing in front of him. "What do you want?" he slurred.

At eleven-thirty in the morning and you've already hit the bottle, are you serious? Sally and Jack produced their IDs.

"Hello, Mr Todd. I'm DI Sally Parker, and this is my partner, DS Jack Blackman. Would it be okay if we came in and spoke to you for a few minutes?"

"What for?" He pulled himself upright. The slight motion proved too much for him, and he staggered against the wall. "Umph. Damn wall just moved," he complained, slurring.

"Are you all right, sir? Maybe it would be better if we went inside to discuss why we're here?"

"No, here will do. Get on with it."

Sally cleared her throat and tucked her warrant card back in her pocket. Jack took out his notebook, just in case Todd uttered anything useful, which Sally doubted was on the cards, given the state of him.

"We're here chasing up information in a possible murder inquiry, sir."

His eyes glazed over. Sally had a feeling they weren't going to get any joy out of him at all.

"Murder? Who? Where? When?" His brow furrowed deeper with each question he spewed out.

"It truly would be better if we came in to speak with you, sir."

His eyelids drooped, and he turned around and staggered up the narrow hallway to the lounge at the rear. "Shut the damn door after you."

Sally left Jack to close the door, and they followed the man into the pit of a lounge. Every surface was littered with newspapers, takeaway cartons, empty bottles and cans. The stench was appalling, too. Body odour and another smell she struggled to distinguish until she surveyed the room and spotted a pile of sick in the corner. Resisting the urge to vomit, Sally crossed the room and flung open the door that led out onto a two-foot-wide balcony which overlooked the car park below.

"Oi, shut that. It's too bloody cold in 'ere to have that open."

"It might be, but it stinks in here. This place is a tip, you should be ashamed of yourself. If the landlord drops by and sees the state of it, he'll more than likely kick you out. Is that what you want?"

He shrugged and snatched up a can of beer from the floor beside him. "Like I give a shit."

"That much is obvious."

She faced her partner. Jack shook his head, cottoning on to what she was about to suggest.

"No way," he mumbled.

"We can't leave him living like this."

"Not our responsibility, boss."

"What are you two whispering about? This is my gaff, I have a right to know," Todd complained, swaying in his seat.

Sally sensed they weren't going to get very far with the man in this condition, but she was finding it hard to quell the need to lend a helping hand. "Is there someone we can call to come and be with you? It's obvious that you need help, sir."

"Nope. They've all turned their backs on me. No fecker wants me around them," he slurred dejectedly.

"May I ask how long you've been in this state?" Sally remained by the open door, sucking in the fresh air in between asking her questions.

"Since Sunday, I suppose," he replied and cackled.

"I meant how many months or years have you been turning to drink for answers."

"Too bloody long. It's the only friend I've got nowadays. None of my so-called friends want to know me, they haven't been near me since she left me for that twat, Swan."

"Since your wife left? Wasn't that over ten years ago?"

"Yep, around then. How do you know?"

"We met your ex-wife and her husband the other day."

His eyes formed tiny slits. "Huh! The pair of cheating fuckers. Pretended they were out there searching for his damn wife, and all the time they were screwing each other's brains out. Sick gits. Not that they're not welcome to each other. But she took everything I owned with her. The house, the car, my life as I knew it, and left me with nothing. They were laughing behind my back for months while I was feeling sorry for him. Disgusting shits, the pair of them. Two peas in a pod, they are."

"Were they having an affair before Jackie went missing? Is that possible?"

"I suppose so. They said they weren't but they're both bloody liars. I wouldn't put it past them."

"Can you cast your mind back for me, to the night Jackie went missing?"

"Yeah, what about it?"

"Can you tell me what went on that night?"

He closed his eyes, and his swaying increased until he snapped them open again. "We were all having fun. I know I was, because Serena was on the other side of the room from

140

me for most of the night, talking to Jackie. They were best friends, always in each other's pockets. That's why she hooked up with him; it floored and sickened me. You wouldn't do that sort of thing to your best friend, would you? Jackie was still classed as missing when she started sleeping with him. It was all too soon, which made me think they were having an affair before that."

"I see. When the Swans were getting ready to leave the party, were there any problems, or couldn't you tell?"

"Problems? Their marriage had been having problems for years." He glanced up, and his eyes widened. "Hey, you don't think he got rid of her... with the intention of nicking my wife, do ya?"

"Is that what you truly believe? Were there signs of them carrying on while Jackie was still around?"

He contemplated the question and took a large swig of beer. "I don't know. I can't think back that far. All I know is they wound up together. It was before that man went down for her murder. All too convenient, the whole kit and caboodle."

Sally cocked her head and asked, "What do you mean by that?"

"One minute they were looking for her, the next they've got someone behind bars. It's not like they found a body, is it? I didn't think the police could convict someone without the body. But then, what do I know? Fuck all, apparently."

"Providing there is enough evidence to convict someone, then yes, we can go ahead and arrest and charge that person."

"Seems like bloody nonsense to me. One minute Jackie was missing, and the next this bloke has been locked up. How does that work?"

"It was a grave mistake."

"No shit! I could have told you that at the time. Like I said, it was all too convenient. It wouldn't surprise me if they were behind her disappearance, but no one investigated that side of things. Plonker that bloke in charge was, a sodding plonker. Anyway, that's by the by, why are you here, questioning me about that night? I don't get it if you've already got someone behind bars for the crime."

Sally sucked in a breath then revealed the truth. "We recently discovered the skeleton of Jackie Swan. Her remains were found buried in the woodland on a nature reserve."

"Where? Not that it matters."

"Thompson Common."

He thought this over for a few seconds and then nodded. "Hmm... not too far from where the party was held that night."

"Yes, we've worked that much out for ourselves. Going back to that night, when Robert and Jackie left the party, did anyone else leave soon after them?"

He blew out a breath. "Now you're asking. How the heck am I supposed to remember that after all these years? Have you spoken to anyone else?"

"Yes, everyone we could find who showed up that night."

"And what did they say?"

"They couldn't really remember."

"There you go then, and you're expecting my boozed-up brain to recall? Not a hope in hell's chance of that happening, lady."

Sally forced out a smile. "It was worth a try. Was there anything about that night that you remember? Anything that you found strange at the time? Did you see Jackie talking to anyone else that night, apart from Serena?"

"Nope. You're asking too much. Serena and Jackie were like glue, stuck to each other all night. Pissed me off at the time, it did, from what I can remember, but what could I do about it? Fuck all, that's what. Do you think they bumped her off and buried her that same night?"

"It's a possibility. We need to go over the details again, searching for possible clues. As yet, we only have assumption on our side, nothing that could substantiate such a claim."

He placed his can on the floor and rubbed his hands together. "It would be good, though, to put them in the spotlight after all these years. Lording it together in that big house of theirs. I'd love to pull the rug from under their smug arses."

"If there's nothing else you can add, we'll leave you to it. Unless you'd like us to lend a hand, getting this place in some sort of order first?"

"Nah! I'm fine. I'll get around to it, one day. I've taken on board what you said about the landlord, and you're right, if he saw the state of this place, I'd be out on my bloody ear. I've had enough of moving around over the years, I'm settled here. I'll clean it up later."

"Good. Thanks for speaking with us today. Stay there, we can show ourselves out."

"You can do me a favour before you leave."

"What's that?"

"Shut that damn door."

Sally chuckled and closed the door to the balcony before she and Jack left the flat. Outside, Jack coughed and doubled over, resting his hands on his knees.

"Fucking hell. That was gross. I didn't think you were ever going to leave."

"I had to try and at least wheedle the information out of him."

"What information could he have possibly flung at us, given the state he was in?" Jack fired back. He stood upright and drew in a lungful of fresh air.

"You're such a cissy, Jack Blackman. Let's get out of here."

He followed her towards the lift. "It's all right for you, you were standing by the open doorway all the time. No thoughts whether I was suffering or not."

"Don't give me that bullshit! You have legs, you could have moved any time you wanted to."

The lift pinged its arrival and ferried them down to the ground floor.

"Where to now?" her partner asked.

"He was the last person we needed to speak to who was at the party. Now I want to go to Jackie's place of work at the time she went missing, see if anything of interest shows up there."

"Makes sense. Wait, there's still a name off the party list we haven't spoken to yet." He flicked through his notes.

Sally pressed the key fob to unlock the car and slipped behind the steering wheel. Jack slid in beside her.

"Who are you talking about?"

"The boss. Now what was his name? It's here somewhere."

"Don't bother, I can remember. It's Grant Calder. I decided to leave him until the end."

"That's because you're a clever dick."

Sally sniggered. "I'll take that as a compliment." She switched on the engine, and the car sparked into life.

"It's the way I intended it. What are your thoughts on the 'happily married couple' now you've spoken to her ex?"

Sally glanced sideways. "Her drunken ex! Let's not lose sight of that when considering what he said during the interview."

"Yeah, I hadn't, don't worry. But there must be an ounce of truth in it somewhere."

"Jury is still out for me. You have to take into account that he's also a very bitter ex who is envious of their new home."

"True enough. Let's hope we get somewhere with her work colleagues then. If they're still working there. You know how much people like to change their jobs these days."

"We'll see. I think some careers are different to others."

SALLY DREW up outside the office of Millmart's Estate Agents around fifteen minutes later. She spoke to the woman on the reception desk. "Hi, I'm DI Parker. Is it possible to speak to the manager or the owner, please?"

The receptionist studied Sally's ID and nodded. "Oh, yes. I'll see if Grant is available." She glanced down at the phone. "He's just put the phone down. I won't be a tick if you'd like to take a seat."

"We're fine, thanks."

The young brunette darted out of her chair and trotted across the room to an office on the far side. She knocked on the door and entered. The door opened again, and she emerged, followed by a man in his early forties. Sally could tell he was wearing a designer suit. His shoes were highly polished, and he fiddled with his cuffs as he walked towards them.

"Hello. I'm Grant Calder. How can I be of assistance? After a property viewing, are you? Want to list your property with us?"

Sally smiled. "Sorry to disappoint you. We're here on police business. We'd rather chat in private if it's all the same to you."

"Sounds ominous. Okay, come through. Would you care for a drink?"

Sally spotted a coffee machine in the corner, behind one of the desks occupied by a blonde woman in her thirties. "A coffee would be wonderful. Milk, one sugar for both of us."

"Gemma, can you do the honours for me and bring them through?"

The blonde nodded and swivelled her chair to deal with the request. Grant opened the door to his office and stepped back to allow Sally and Jack to enter. He raced around his desk and raised a finger, preventing Sally from speaking when the super-efficient Gemma entered the room with three cups.

"I made you one as well, Grant."

"Thanks, Gemma. Close the door on your way out, will you?"

Gemma smiled and backed up. The door thudded shut behind her.

"Now that we're alone, how can I help?" Grant said.

"We're from the Cold Case Unit."

His eyebrow shot up, and he reached for his coffee and took a sip. "Go on. That doesn't really tell me much."

"What about if I add that we're here to try and find out what happened to Jackie Swan?"

His eyes widened, and he shifted in his seat. "I don't understand. Why are you still digging into her case when the killer is already confined to a cell in prison?"

"You may well ask. Unfortunately, or fortunately for her family, depending on how you look at it, Jackie's remains were discovered this week."

He sat forward and then promptly turned sideways to vomit in his wastepaper bin. Whilst still bent over, he snatched open several drawers until he found what he was looking for, a tissue. Then he proceeded to wipe his mouth. Sally and Jack glanced at each other. Sally frowned and drew her attention back to Grant.

"Grant, are you okay?"

He sat upright and ran the tissue over his mouth several times; each time seemed to be more aggressive than the last. "Sorry. It was such a shock to hear you say that. I don't think any of us expected to ever hear that news. Where? Where was she found?" He wiped his mouth again, folded the tissue into four and then dabbed at his eyes. After which he threw it in the bin beside him, grimacing at the contents he'd deposited in it a few seconds earlier.

"A grave was uncovered at Thompson Common by workmen planting trees."

"Oh my. What a shock it must have been for them."

"Indeed."

"But I still don't understand why you're reinvestigating the case after all this time, if that's why you're here."

"Let me give you some background. Our team has been inspecting all the cases that were investigated by Inspector Falkirk. Jackie's case was one of those in question."

"But why? I can't seem to get my head around this."

"It has come to our attention over the last couple of years that Inspector Falkirk had an agenda."

"An agenda?" He paused and then pointed at her. "Oh God, are you telling me he was bent?"

"Yes. Therefore, every case he's ever worked on has had to be reopened and reinvestigated."

"Jesus! You see this sort of thing going on in the movies, but really, I didn't know it happened in real life. Are you telling me there are people sitting in prison who were totally innocent of the crimes they were supposed to have committed?"

"Yes. Over the last couple of years, since the unit was formed, we've been doing our very best to set these people free. I have to tell you, we've succeeded in quite a few of the cases. Unfortunately, in Gordon Dawson's case, it has come too late."

Grant frowned. "Dawson? Oh no, it's all coming back to me now. Wasn't he the one who was accused of Jackie's murder?"

"That's right. Mr Dawson died a few years ago."

He shrugged. "Just because he snuffed it, it doesn't mean he didn't kill her."

"Which is why we've reopened the case. The thing is that Gordon Dawson has always denied killing Jackie. Even on his deathbed, his final words were that he had been wronged and that he never even met Jackie, let alone killed her."

"That's terrible. But he was a convicted criminal, do you tend to take the word of a man locked up like that? Sorry if that's a dumb question."

"It isn't. As I said, we've been investigating a number of old cases and found several unsafe convictions. That has prompted us to err on the side of caution with the other investigations Falkirk was involved in. Had Jackie's body remained undiscovered then I suppose we would have left things alone. However, as the case has been highlighted again, we've been trawling through the evidence, at the same time shaking our heads in disbelief that Dawson was ever convicted of the crime."

"How strange. What happens now? What about any evidence gathering? How will that be obtained?"

"Through police work along with any forensic clues that have remained in the grave with the victim."

He shot forward in his chair, showing more interest in the subject than Sally had thought likely. "How fascinating. What sort of evidence?"

Sally raised a finger. "I'm afraid I can't possibly say any more on that front. Sorry."

He sat back again, and his shoulders slumped. "That's a shame. Of course, it is totally understandable in the circumstances. What can I do for you specifically today?"

"We'd like to go over your statement and possibly talk to the other members of your staff."

"Geez, you're expecting us to remember the events of around the time Jackie was taken from us?"

"As best as you can. It's surprising what the memory can

recall in instances such as this," Sally replied, bearing in mind how well Denis had just fared in his drunken stupor.

"Glad you have faith in what's up here." He smiled and jabbed at the side of his head.

"Okay, shall we begin? Jack will take notes while I ask the questions, if that's all right?"

"Sure. What do you want to know?"

"How well you knew Jackie."

Grant picked up his silver pen from the desk and began winding it through his fingers as he spoke. "Well, as well as any boss knows a member of staff, I suppose. She was one of our best negotiators at the time. It was a great loss when she left us, not only because she was a close friend to all of us, but because the business declined for a few months after her disappearance. So much so that I was hauled over the coals by head office." He grinned. "It doesn't take them much to get on a manager's back, as you can imagine. Lacking in empathy and compassion, that lot. Here we all were, struggling to make sense of why Jackie would up and leave like that, and all the time they were on the phone daily, telling me to pull my finger out."

"Sorry to hear that. How did you survive the pressure?"

"That was easy enough, once it was determined that Dawson had been arrested and charged months later, for murdering Jackie. Someone came down from head office, one of the directors, it was. He made a right fuss. Took me out to dinner as a form of apology. They even stuck their hands in their pockets and gave me and every member of the team a five-hundred-pound bonus that Christmas. We were all gobsmacked but appreciated the gesture. Not that they should have come down heavy on us in the first place. It was guilt money on their part. The staff all kicked up a fuss, they wanted to reject the payment at first. I told them if they did that, head office would probably think twice about dishing out any bonuses due in the near future."

"I agree. You have to be so careful you don't shoot your-self in the foot."

"Exactly. Anyway, we got past it, but the agency never felt the same again after she went."

"I can understand why, if Jackie was well liked. According to our records, you were there that night. At the party, weren't you?"

He scratched his head. "The night she supposedly went missing, yes? That's right. Why?"

"I was wondering if you could go through the events of the evening for us, if you wouldn't mind."

"What's to tell? We were celebrating the anniversary of mutual friends."

"Did you go with someone? A significant other?"

His head tilted, and he glanced at the wall behind Sally for a few moments and then returned his gaze to her. "Thinking back, no, I went alone. It was around the time I had split up with Samantha, my long-term girlfriend. I caught her cheating on me. Jackie was a good listener. I told her that I didn't want to attend the party, she said that would be foolish and our friends wouldn't think anything of it if I turned up alone. In truth, on the night, I felt like a spare prick at a wedding."

"But Jackie was there, you could have joined up with her for the evening, couldn't you?"

He batted away the suggestion. "Nope. She was too wrapped up with Serena to even care."

Sally detected a bitterness in his tone.

He laughed. "At least, I think that's what happened, I suppose my memory isn't as good as it should be about that evening. I seem to recall it had been a hectic week around here. I busted a gut to close an important deal on one of our more exclusive properties that day before I attended the party. It was one of Jackie's, she should have been here that night but she didn't want to let her friends down. She tried to persuade me to leave the transaction until the morning, but the clients were expecting it to be tied down by the end of the day because they were jetting off to... where was it...? Ah, yes, somewhere like Mauritius."

"I see. Needs must in that case. Did it cause a rift between you and Jackie?"

"Er, no. Not that I can remember. The deal meant that the office earnt over fifty grand in commission from that sale. I was buzzing when I got to the party. I tried to share the news with Jackie, but she was caught up with Serena. I decided to leave it until we were at work the next day, thought I'd share it with the rest of the team at the same time. Except, Jackie didn't show up for work. It kind of spoilt our excitement. The biggest deal the office had ever accomplished, and we couldn't celebrate it together."

"Ouch, that must have hurt."

"Yes and no. I suppose it's like everything in life, we all have to deal with disappointments now and then. That happened to be one of the major ones in my life. I got over it, eventually. Mustn't be maudlin about it, you don't want to hear about my grievances."

Sally smiled. "It's okay. It's always interesting to learn how a business like this ticks over. What about the rest of the staff, how did they react to the news of Jackie going missing?"

"They were in shock for weeks. So frustrating at the time, I couldn't get any work out of them. She was my eyes and ears out there, you see. Geed the girls up if they were slacking during the day. A huge motivator."

"I get it. Hence the performance of the branch taking a nosedive after she went missing."

"That's correct. It was extremely difficult to get things back on track. It took a few months, but we got there in the end."

"May I ask how? Did someone take over Jackie's position?"

"Not as such. I called a meeting and laid it on the line with everyone, told them their jobs were in danger if they didn't pull their fingers out. At first, they were pissed off by the threat, but what they didn't realise was that head office were ringing me daily, sometimes three to four times a day. It put me under extreme pressure, I can tell you. In the end, I had to come down heavy on them to save my own job."

"Bosses can be so demanding when targets aren't met, we appreciate that fact. It's the same in the police force."

He nodded. "I can imagine. Anyway, all that's in the past now. We got through it. That's the main thing. The agency got back on course, and to this day, we're still the best branch this side of the country."

"Excellent news. You must be so chuffed. Going back to the party. Did you observe Jackie that night?"

"Observe? Are you asking if I spied on her?"

"Sorry, poor choice of words. From a distance, did you see anything out of the ordinary happening that night with Jackie?"

"If I knew what you were asking, I could possibly answer. Can you try to be more specific for me?"

"Yes, okay. Did Jackie have any problems during the evening? Possibly with one of the other partygoers?"

He chewed on his lip and placed a clenched hand under his chin as he contemplated the question. "Again, you're testing my memory, and I can't really give you a definitive answer. As far as I can remember, Serena and Jackie were stuck together all evening."

"Yes, okay. That's what we've been led to believe. Can you

tell me what time you left the party that night? Just roughly, was it before or after the Swans went home?"

"Again, I'm going to have to dig deep. Ah, yes, I think it was just after they left. There was a slight atmosphere between Jackie and Robert, it ended up turning the evening sour, as far as I can recall."

"Okay, I think we've heard enough. I wonder if it would be an imposition if we spoke to the rest of the staff, while we're here today."

"I don't have a problem with that. Please ensure it doesn't take too long. Some of the ladies have a couple of clients to see later on. If you can work around the appointments already in place, then I have no objection."

"Is there a room we can use to carry out the interviews?"

"Yes. The restroom, it's small, maybe too small for your needs. Other than that, I could gather a few things together and you could use my office, providing you don't spend all day in here."

"That would be perfect. I appreciate you bending over backwards to help with our enquiries."

He smiled and nodded. "It's my pleasure. The least I can do in the circumstances. If it helps you uncover what you need then that's got to be seen as an added bonus. Who do you want to see first?"

"Shall we go with seniority? Obviously working around the appointments you already have in place."

"I'll make the arrangements while you finish your drinks. Bear with me for five minutes or so."

He left the room. Sally and Jack drank the rest of their drinks and mulled over what they'd heard.

"Nothing springing to mind for me. What about you?" Sally asked her partner.

"Nope. Nothing as yet. You know what we're lacking for this investigation?"

Sally tilted her head. "No, pray share it with me, if you will?"

He rolled his eyes at her patronising tone. "I could always keep my mouth shut instead."

Sally grinned. "I'm messing with you. Go on, I'm all ears."

"All right. Stating the obvious, bloody CCTV footage. I know, I know, the incident took place out in the lanes, but maybe we could have picked up the car on the cameras in town when the couple were driving through and seen if anyone was following them."

"Yep, that horse bloody bolted years ago, Jack. No point dwelling on what we don't have to hand, is there?"

"All right, it was just something I needed to air with you."

The door opened, and Grant returned to the room, accompanied by a smartly dressed brunette lady.

"This is Fiona, she's been working for me since the branch opened, almost twenty years now. I'll just gather a few files and leave you to it. Make yourself at home in my chair, Fiona. Don't get too comfortable, though." He smiled and collected the manilla folders in his in-tray.

Sally smiled. "Thanks again for allowing us to use your office, Grant. We'll be as quick as we can."

"No problem. I hope it all goes well." He left the office and closed the door softly behind him.

Fiona strolled around the desk and settled into her boss's chair. "Blimey, I might never want to leave. Why do bosses always have the better equipment and yet it's the workers who get all the work done?"

Sally laughed. "Don't get me started on that one. Did Grant tell you what this interview is about?"

A sadness descended over Fiona. "Yes, I never thought this subject would be raised again, not after all these years. I can't believe Jackie's finally been discovered. I feel for Robert, although I hear he's already moved on with his life. I bet news like this will throw a spanner in the works between him and Serena." Fiona's tone changed from one filled with compassion to one of acrimony by the end of her statement.

Sally's interest gene went on the alert. "Oh? Why would you think that?"

She leaned back in the comfy chair. "Think about it... they put Jackie's death to bed years ago. I doubt if either of them has given her much thought over the years. Too busy being loved-up, I'm guessing."

"I take it you know Robert and Serena well?"

"Sort of, but only through what Jackie told me. I was shocked to see they were an item during the media's attention into the court case."

"Did Jackie ever mention if their marriage was in strife?"

Fiona paused to think. "Not really. Although she did mention that things had changed between her and Robert."

"When was this?"

"A few months before she went missing, I believe."

"Did she go into further detail?" Sally asked, sitting forward at the snippet of news.

"No. She didn't really confide in me. She had Serena for that. Anyway, she had enough problems to worry about going on around here."

"Sorry? Can you elucidate?"

"It was around that time that Ned Buckland was making her life a misery."

Sally snatched her head around to look at Jack. "Does that name ring a bell?"

Jack's brow furrowed. "No, not at all."

"You're going to need to tell us more. Who was he?"

"Ned worked here as a negotiator for a while."

"When did he leave?"

Fiona looked at the ceiling as she thought. "Probably a

few months before Jackie went missing, as far as I can remember."

"How was he making her life a misery?"

"God, now you're asking." She paused for a moment or two and then snapped her finger and thumb together. "It was over a massive mansion we had on file. The woman owner didn't get on with Ned and requested that Jackie take over from him during the negotiations. That pissed him off, and he started throwing his toys out of the pram. At least, that's how I remember it. Maybe the other girls will be able to help out more. You've got to take into account how much time has passed since this all happened."

"Believe me, I appreciate just how long it has been. You said her marriage was in trouble a few months before she went missing. Do you think the stress of the situation with the Ned problem affected her home life as well?"

Fiona shrugged. "Who knows? It was too long ago."

"That's okay, you've given us something else to look into. What about the customers or clients? Was there anyone around that time who might have been causing problems for Jackie? Someone keen to only deal with her? Aside from the woman who owned the mansion."

Another shake of the head. "I don't think so, but I could be wrong. It's just too far back to recall, sorry."

"Not to worry. Is there anything else you think we should know?"

"Not that I can think of, sorry."

"It's okay. You can go now. Would you mind sending in the next person?"

Fiona smiled, pushed back in the chair and walked out of the room.

Sally glanced over her shoulder and waited for the door to close. "Sounds like we need to track down this Ned Buckland, he could be a key part of this investigation."

"As in a prime suspect?"

"Possibly, although I want to swerve thinking that for now, at least. He's still someone we need to have a chat with all the same. As soon as we leave here, we'll give Joanna a ring, ask her to try and find him for us."

"Maybe someone else will be able to tell us where he moved to after leaving here and if he's still in the area."

There was a slight knock on the door. "Come in," Sally shouted.

A slim redhead entered the room and sat in the seat opposite. Her cheeks matched the colour of her hair. "Hi, I'm Lyndsey Collins. You wanted to see me?"

Sally sensed the woman didn't want to be there by the way her hands were fidgeting in front of her. One minute they were clutched together, the next they were thrust apart, and that all took place before Sally had even spoken.

"Hi, Lyndsey. Please, there's no need to feel nervous, we're just here for a quick chat. It shouldn't take long."

"That's okay. Sorry, I've never been asked to speak with the police before, so you'll have to forgive my hesitancy in places."

"Just relax, we're not all ogres, I promise you. Has Grant explained what this interview is about?"

She let out a hitched breath. "Yes, he mentioned that you had discovered Jackie's remains after all these years. I'm pleased you have, her poor family must have gone through hell, not knowing if she was actually dead or alive. I thought it was very strange when that copper arrested that man, without finding her body. Is that common?"

"No, not really. Inspector Falkirk believed he was doing the right thing at the time. The man had also killed two other women in the area a few months prior to his arrest."

"So he was the prime suspect in other suspicious acts, is

that what you're telling me? Sorry, I'm trying to figure out how all of this works."

"Yes, that about sums it up. Did you know Jackie well?"

"Yes, as well as one colleague would know another but, if you're asking if we were best friends, then I would have to say no."

"But there was no animosity between you?"

Lyndsey frowned and seemed horrified by the suggestion. "No, definitely not. Why do you ask?"

"Bear with me, all I'm trying to ascertain is why she was killed. We believe the man who was sentenced for her murder was innocent and the true culprit was allowed to go free. Hence the reason we are here today and the necessity for us to reopen the investigation into the crime after all these years."

She gasped and covered her mouth with a hand, which she dropped after a few moments. "How terrible for her family to go through all this again. To drag everything back up after all these years. Have you spoken to Robert?"

"We have. While he's upset that we've found his former wife's remains, he's just as keen to find out who her murderer is."

Her head inclined. "You're not suggesting it could have been one of us, are you?"

Sally smiled. "I'm not suggesting anything of the sort, however, we're here today to see if any of her former work colleagues can help us out. By possibly recalling if there was anything troubling Jackie at around the time of her disappearance."

"Ah, yes. I understand now. What did Fiona tell you?"

"I'd rather not go into detail. I need your account of what took place back then, if you understand what I'm asking?"

Lyndsey chewed on her cherry-coloured lips and stared

down at her linked hands, rubbing one thumb up and down the other. "Did she tell you about Ned?"

"His name did crop up. Would you care to tell me more?"

"He got snarky with Jackie over a rich client's property. Not long after it all kicked off, he left and went to work for a competitor."

"That's what Fiona told us. Can you tell us the name of the competitor?"

"Bradshaw and Co. They're situated around the corner."

"And when he left, do you know if Jackie ever saw him again?"

She shook her head. "I'm not sure. She may have done and not bothered to mention it. We still see him, you know, pass him in the street now and again."

Sally's interest soared once more. "Ah, so he still works at the same agency to this day?"

"Oh yes. He's their top negotiator. Actually, I spoke to him the other day. He seems very chilled. Was bragging about his new penthouse flat in an exclusive development in Norwich. I noticed he was driving around in a Porsche as well. Yes, I'd say he's done very well for himself."

"Okay, we'll be sure to have a chat with him after we leave here. What about clients? Was there any trouble there?"

"With Ned or with Jackie?"

"Sorry, I should have made it clearer, with Jackie."

Releasing her hands, she ran a finger across her bottom lip. "There's something at the back of my mind, can you give me a second?"

"Of course. Take your time."

Lyndsey's finger tapped at her lip, and her eyes narrowed. "Wait a second, yes, I remember now. There was this chap who was going through a divorce. He came in looking for a property, and Jackie was her usual friendly self and went through a couple of possible options with him. I believe he

159

ended up buying a cottage out at Acle or somewhere out that way." She smiled. "Once he was settled, he walked in here with this ginormous bouquet of flowers for Jackie."

"How did Jackie react?"

"She was dreadfully embarrassed by the man's generosity. It wasn't until he left that she shuddered and said she didn't want them. I said she must be crazy, and she fell silent. I didn't want to push it any further, not in front of the others. I took the flowers out the back for her. She joined me and flopped into the chair next to me and whispered, 'You don't understand. He tried it on with me. I had to slap him down while I was showing him around the cottage'. She turned green while she was telling me, as though she wanted to vomit."

"Did the man ever contact her again?"

"Yes, he rang a few times. Asked her out to lunch one day. She turned him down, of course. I remember it got to the point that she was scared to answer her phone when it rang."

"That must have been horrendous for her. How long did his attention towards her last, can you recall?"

"A few weeks at least. In the end, Grant had to step in and take his calls. They soon stopped."

"Can you remember when this took place?"

"A few months before her disappearance. Maybe around six months even. I can look it up for you, if you like?"

"That would be wonderful."

"I'll do it now. I'll be right back." She tore out of the office.

"I don't remember reading anything about a customer coming on too strong, do you?" Sally asked, the second the coast was clear.

Jack tutted. "Nope. I'm not surprised. Falkirk was a prime tosser. Probably spent most of his time propping up the bar at the nearest pub rather than doing the legwork needed to crack a case."

"You're probably right. Coming here has certainly proved productive so far. Let's hope it leads to a suspect."

Lyndsey returned and handed Sally a sheet of paper. On it was the name Patrick Gower and an address. "It's all I have. Not sure if he still lives there or not."

"And he was going through a divorce at the time?"

"Yes, that's right."

"We'll look into it. Thanks for this, it could be a huge help. Is there anyone else you can think of?"

Lyndsey was still standing in front of her. "No, I don't think so. That's the only one who stuck out in my memory. Is there anything else you need from me?"

"No. You've been really helpful. I'm grateful for the information you've provided us with today."

"My pleasure. I hope it helps solve the riddle of Jackie's death and gives her family some form of closure. Hasn't Robert got married again?"

"Yes, that's right."

She smiled and walked back towards the door.

"Could you send the next person in, please?" Sally shouted over her shoulder.

"Okay, that'll be Gemma." The door closed behind her.

"We need to try and get hold of Gower's ex-wife. Get the lowdown on his background as soon as we leave here."

"If you don't mind taking the notes with the next one, I could nip outside and get the ball rolling on what we need."

"All right, you do that. We could do with the backgrounds on both Ned and this Gower fella. Also, once you've contacted Joanna, give Bradshaw's a call, see if Ned is around this morning. We might as well drop by and see him after we've finished here, it would be remiss of us not to as we're on the doorstep."

"Leave it with me. Here's my notebook and pen. Can you remember how it works, you know, taking notes down?"

Sally pulled a face at him. "Smartarse. Go and make yourself useful for a change."

"Bloody cheek. It was my idea to try and save time. Funny how you conveniently forgot that fact."

"Yadda, yadda. Get out of my hair, man," Sally called after him good-naturedly.

He opened the door and apologised to the woman he almost bumped into. "Sorry. Here you go." Jack stepped back to allow the woman into the room.

Sally swivelled in her seat. "Come and join me. Don't mind my partner, he's on a mission."

"Oh, right. Okay. I'm Gemma Knight," the blonde said, taking a seat. "Nice chair, first time I've been allowed to sit in it. I feel honoured."

"I'll let Grant know." Sally sniggered.

"Oh God, no, please don't say anything."

Sally frowned. "May I ask why?"

Gemma rolled her eyes. "His sense of humour died years ago. We tend to walk around here on eggshells most of the time."

"Is that true? He didn't come across as a grouchy boss."

"Looks can be deceptive," she grumbled. "Let's just say he has good days and bad days."

Sally smiled to put the woman at ease. "My boss is the same. I tend to steer clear of him most days if I can help it."

Gemma returned her smile. "Grant told us why you're here. I'm glad you've finally found Jackie. We didn't get along when we worked together, but I still wouldn't wish what happened to her on my worst enemy."

"Care to tell me more about your relationship?" Sally jotted down notes as Gemma spoke.

"I always regarded her as conceited. The others didn't, so maybe it was just me who thought that."

"May I ask why?"

Gemma sighed and leaned back in the plush chair. She bounced forward again when she sank too low and wriggled back in her seat. "There was no doubting that she was good at her job, but there are some people who simply put their head down and get on with it. Not Jackie, she made sure everyone knew she'd met the targets Grant set us at the beginning of the month, long before anyone else did."

"She taunted you with the fact, is that what you're telling me?"

"Yes. Shoved our noses in it. Most people would slacken off, maybe hand any extra work over to their colleagues to help raise their profile a bit in Grant's eyes, but no, not Jackie. She continued to go hell for leather to get even more money coming in, for herself. That stuck in my throat. At the time, I remember having a go at her. Told her what I thought of her when the others just sat there and said nothing. Grant brought us both into this very office and gave us a good talking-to—no, let me correct myself, he gave *me* a good talking-to while she stood there with a huge smirk on her face."

"There was no love lost between the two of you then?"

"No. Definitely not. I think Ned felt the same way when he was here, too. There always appeared to be a touch of favouritism from Grant towards Jackie. They socialised together, you see."

"Ah, I get it. Is that why Ned left?"

"Yep, there was that incident with a rich customer. She didn't get along with Ned and warmed to Jackie when she came in here one day. That's when she switched negotiators and asked to be teamed up with Jackie. Ned was rightly livid, but instead of complaining about it, he decided to throw in the towel and go elsewhere. I was teetering on the edge of doing it myself around that time, too, but decided to stay and plod on. Truth be told, I thought my bonuses would go up each month if there was one less negotiator as competition."

"And did it?"

"Not initially, no. Jackie took on the extra workload, dealing with Ned's customers."

"What? His portfolio of customers wasn't divided equally between the remaining staff?"

"Nope. Shocking, right?"

Sally frowned. "Yes, to me that's uncalled for and goes against the grain, and yet, you're still here today, despite this all taking place, what, twelve years ago?"

"I know." She sighed heavily. "Glutton for punishment, that's me. However, things settled down considerably after Jackie disappeared. Grant started pulling his weight more, took over the better houses we had on our books; maybe he felt guilty sitting in this office all day every day, I don't know."

"Was that fair of him? Wouldn't it have been fairer for him to have divided the customers between the rest of you?"

"Maybe. At the time, we were all in shock about what had happened to Jackie, even more so when that bloke was arrested for her murder and banged up. Grant announced the news and told us justice had been done, at last."

"And everyone got back to normal, just like that?"

Gemma picked up a pen and ran her fingers up and down it. "I suppose so. Everything was far more chilled around here than before… you know, Jackie went missing."

"So tensions were fraught most of the time?"

"Most of the time would be inaccurate, possibly part of the time."

"Did you and Jackie ever come to blows?"

"No, things never got that bad between us, the other girls and Grant would have stepped in and prevented that from happening. We tolerated each other, I can't say any more than that, not really."

"Is there anything else you can tell us about the time Jackie went missing?"

She put the pen down and shook her head. "Nope, that's all I can tell you. I have an enquiring mind, so you'll have to forgive me for asking this: what state was the body in, after all these years? The reason I'm asking is that I watch a lot of the true crime documentaries on the TV and, well..."

"Jackie's remains were in the form of a skeleton. I'd rather you not reveal that to the others, though, it might upset them."

"I get it. Wow, I suppose I half-expected you to say that, but that's crazy to hear. I bet Robert was distraught when he heard the news."

"Mixed emotions, I suppose. Distraught and relieved at the same time."

"Not casting aspersions on the poor man, but I thought it strange that he should link up with her best friend. Oh, ignore me. Now I've said that out loud, it sounds wrong to mention it."

"A source of comfort for both of them. Apparently, they both searched for Jackie for months. My guess is they spent a long time together and feelings developed between them."

"Yeah, I bet that's what happened. Good luck to them, it would have been wrong for him not to have pounced on the chance of happiness when it dropped into his lap."

"I agree. Right, I think we're done here now. Thanks for your insight into things."

She rose from her seat. "You're welcome. I hope it helps to catch the real killer. Has the man in prison been set free now?"

"No, sadly he died a few years ago."

"Oh my, such a shame for him and his poor family."

"Yes. There's not a lot else I can say, except to vow we find the real killer. Although, he was a convicted killer anyway."

"Ah, I get you. I hope you succeed in your mission."

Sally followed Gemma out of the room and into the outer office. Grant was lingering by the door, talking to someone on the phone.

"Okay, mate. I've got to go. I'll give you a buzz later." He prodded the button to end the call and slipped off the desk he had been perched on. "All finished now? Can I reclaim my office?"

She smiled. "You can. I can't thank you and your staff enough for talking to us today, it's been rather enlightening."

"Oh?" He tilted his head to the left. "Care to fill me in on what my staff have been telling you?"

Sally tapped the side of her nose. "Sorry, more than I dare do. Thanks again. I'll leave a few of my cards with you. If you or any of your staff can think of anything else, please, give me a call."

"We will. I'll pass them around. Will you keep us updated on how the investigation is going?"

"We don't generally do that, only with members of the family."

"I see."

"Thanks again, Grant." She held out a hand, and he shook it firmly.

Sally left the agency and joined Jack who was still on the phone.

"Hang on, Joanna, the boss is here. I'll put you on speaker."

"Hello, boss. I was just saying that I've managed to track down Patrick Gower's ex-wife. Her address is fifty-six Cotton Road, Wymondham. So just around the corner from the station."

"That's brilliant news. We're going to call and see Ned first." She glanced at her partner as if confirming that to be the case. Jack nodded and gave her the thumbs-up. "Then we'll drop by Gower's place and also see what his ex has to say before we head back to the station."

"Sounds like a plan. In the meantime, I'll keep digging, and if anything should show up, I'll either ring you or send you a text."

"Do that. Have Lorne and Jordan set off yet?"

"They're getting ready to leave now. Do you want a quick word with her?"

"Yes, thanks, Jo."

"Just a second. Lorne, the boss wants a word in your shell-like."

Lorne came on the line. "Hello."

"I just wanted to send you on your way with my best wishes. I hope the visit goes according to plan. I forgot to mention, if you can, try and arrange a visit behind a Perspex screen so he can't get his hands on either Natalie or the baby."

"I never thought about that. Leave it with me. I'll make sure it happens. Dare I ask how you and Jack have got on there?"

"We have a few things we have to check into, a couple of possible suspects and iffy scenarios we need to verify. Just heading off to see a former colleague of Jackie's who left because there was a frosty atmosphere between him and Jackie. We'll see how it goes."

"Good luck. Maybe we can meet up later, possibly over dinner, and compare notes. What do you say?"

"Sounds great to me. My place or yours?"

"Ours would be better, what with you and Simon being out all day and Tony sat at home… I was going to add doing nothing, but that simply isn't true."

"He's a treasure. We'll firm up our plans later."

"Speak soon. Cracking on."

Sally handed the phone back to her partner and surveyed the street.

Jack ended the call with Joanna and pointed to the right. "Bradshaw's is around the corner. We'd better make it snappy, the woman said Ned had an appointment he needed to get to in an hour."

Sally grinned. "What are we waiting for then?"

The agency was laid out much the same as the one they'd just visited. It was predominantly manned by women in their thirties to forties, although the older generation was represented by a lady with grey hair, tucked away in the rear corner.

Sally and Jack produced their IDs, and Sally spoke to the woman at the desk nearest to the door.

"Sorry to disturb you, is Ned Buckland around, please?"

"Oh, the police? Umm... yes, I believe he's in the back office with the manager. I can go and get him for you. Can I ask what your visit is about? He's bound to ask me."

Nice try. Sally smiled. "It's personal."

"I'll be sure to tell him that. If you'd like to wait here, I won't be long." The woman left her chair under the inquisitive gazes of the other members of staff and knocked on the office towards the rear.

A man's voice bellowed for her to enter. She dipped inside and came out a few seconds later followed by two men, one in his late thirties, dressed in a pinstriped suit, and the other, a much older man in a tweed jacket, who had thin gold spectacles perched on the end of his nose.

"What's the meaning of this visit?" asked the older man.

Sally flashed her ID again and added a smile. "Sorry to interrupt your meeting, gents. We'd like a brief chat with Mr Buckland, if you don't mind?"

"Concerning what?" the older gent demanded, his face flushing in anger.

"It's a personal matter." Sally turned her attention to Ned. "Is there somewhere private we can go?"

Ned appeared to be as confused as his boss. "I suppose we could use the staffroom out the back."

"Yes, do that. Don't forget you've got that very important meeting in less than fifty minutes, Ned."

"I won't, Mr Charles. Hopefully this won't take long." He gestured for Sally and Jack to follow him and led them through the door at the rear of the office and along a short corridor to a room no bigger than ten by ten, kitted out with a table with four chairs and a small kitchen area over to the left. Ned pulled out one of the chairs and sat. "Perhaps you wouldn't mind telling me what this is about, and if it's a personal issue, why in God's name you've come to see me here rather than call at my home?"

Sally and Jack sat opposite him. Jack withdrew his notebook from his jacket pocket and opened it.

"First of all, I'd like to thank you for agreeing to see us, it makes things a lot easier," Sally said.

"Easier? Why would I object to talking to the police? Can we get on with this? I'm on a tight schedule as it is, dancing around the issue isn't going to help."

"Okay. I'm in charge of the Norfolk Constabulary Cold Case Unit. We're investigating a crime that was committed over twelve years ago."

He slammed back in his chair. "What? Not the Jackie Swan case?"

"That's the one. New evidence has come our way this week, which has forced us to reinvestigate the case."

He bounced forward again, his eyebrow cocked with interest. "What new evidence?"

"A skeleton was found and has since been identified as Jackie Swan."

He left his chair and raced over to the sink where he

ran the water and splashed it over his face. Grabbing the hand towel hanging from a ring on the wall, he turned to face them. "Jesus, are you bloody serious? After all this time?"

"Yes. She was formally identified by her husband."

He shook his head in disbelief. "I'm finding this extremely hard to process. Why? How? Do things like this even happen? When that bloke was charged with her murder, I thought it was a bloody mistake."

"May I ask why?"

"Umm... the fact there wasn't a body for a start. Jesus, I'm struggling with this." He staggered back to his chair and slumped into it. "To say you've shocked me would be the understatement of the millennium. How does one recover the body of someone after all this time?"

"That's not our concern at present. Obviously, with the emergence of her remains, we have been forced to revisit the crime."

"Why, when someone is already serving time for her murder? I don't get it."

"We've been investigating several cases that were carried out by DI Falkirk. Unfortunately, some of them were what we would call 'unsafe convictions'."

His eyes widened. "What? He laid crimes at innocent peoples' doors just for the sake of it? Is that what you're telling me?"

"Apparently so. We've investigated dozens of crimes and set some prisoners free because of lack of, or what we considered, false evidence."

"That's deplorable. How are people supposed to trust our legal system if you guys are intent on stitching people up?"

Sally raised her finger. "Just to clarify, not all coppers are bent."

"No, I don't suppose they are. But you coming here today,

telling me that someone else went down for Jackie's murder, has blown me away."

"It is what it is. We're here to redress the wrongs that have been committed over the years. I have a few questions, if I may? We've just visited Millmart's Estate Agents, your former employer."

He chuckled. "I'm aware of who they are, Inspector. What about it?"

"During a couple of interviews with the staff, your name cropped up. We're here today to ask for your side of the events that led up to you leaving your previous job."

"It's simple. I was forced out."

"In what way? Would you mind telling us why you believe that to be the case?"

"In every way possible. Grant was, and always will be, a prick in my opinion."

"Why?"

Ned stared at his hands which were clenched into tight fists. "He didn't run that office fairly."

"Did you report the issue to head office?"

He glanced up and laughed. "What would be the point? His uncle owns the business."

Everything suddenly slotted into place. *Why wouldn't Grant have told us?* "Ah, we weren't aware of that."

"There you go, you obviously haven't asked the right people. The other staff suck up to him for fear of losing their jobs most days, I shouldn't wonder. It has always been the same."

"Things were bad when you worked there then, is that correct?"

"Yes. And do you know why?"

"No." Sally grinned. "But I have a feeling you're going to tell us."

"Too right I am. It's sexism from the other side. Because

I've got dangly bits between my legs, that's what he objected to. He ruled the office through fear and equal amounts of praise. If that makes sense?"

Sally waved her hand from side to side. "I think I know what you're getting at, but go on."

"Either the girls did as they were told or they were out on their ears. He set unrealistic targets, that were mostly unachievable, to keep people in line."

"But Jackie didn't have a problem meeting those targets, month after month, did she?"

He cocked an eyebrow. "You know about that?"

"Yes, a member of staff gave us the lowdown on how the bonuses worked out."

"I bet they didn't tell you that it was Grant who organised the staff's weekly schedule, did they?"

"I'm not with you. Meaning?"

"He gave Jackie all the plum clients. The leads that were bound to end up in a sale. While the rest of us were given the ones most people would recognise as time-wasters."

"Ah, okay, I understand now. So nailed-on certainties to end up in a sale. Did you get many of those during the week?"

"At least five or six back in the day. That was a lot of dosh we're talking about, even back then."

"Didn't you ever raise the point with Grant?"

He held his hands up. "Why bother? He wouldn't have changed anything. He favoured Jackie, everyone could see that."

Sally's suspicious gene prodded her. "May I ask why?"

"Probably because he wanted to get into her knickers."

"Is that bitterness speaking or is it the truth?"

"It's a fact, a solid gold one."

"How do you know that? Did you ever tackle him about it?"

"Jackie told me."

Sally shuffled forward in her seat. "What? She came right out and told you he'd made a play for her?"

"Yep. We confided in each other."

Another revelation that was a sucker punch to her stomach. "You were close friends and confidants? Is that what you're telling me?"

"Yes. Although we didn't let on at work."

"See, this is where I'm confused. We were led to believe that you left under a cloud and that you had some form of grudge against Jackie, and here you are telling us that you were good friends."

"We were much more than that, Inspector."

Sally gulped. "Care to enlighten us as to the level of your relationship? Were you having an affair?" Sally revisited what the staff at the previous agency had said about Ned. *Some people pretend to hate each other at work, in an attempt to put their work colleagues off the scent of an affair. Is this what happened between Ned and Jackie?*

He laughed. "It's not what you think."

"What was it then?"

He sucked in a large breath. "She was my half-sister."

Boom! What a bloody revelation.

"Ah, I see. And you kept the fact hidden from the rest of the staff because you thought there might be more favouritism from Grant if he found out you were related."

He shook his head. "It wasn't because of that. Honestly, I can't remember why we decided to do it, but it didn't take me long to suss out Grant had an agenda with Jackie."

"Did Jackie ever tackle him about the issue?"

"I believe she slapped him down once or twice."

"Oh, really? This is all news to us. Can you share with us how far things went between them?"

"Jackie told me they were at the office one night, working

173

late, and he ran a hand up her leg. When she told me, I threatened to go round there and batter him. She warned me that if I did that, there was a chance we could both lose our jobs."

"How did she combat the issue?"

"She talked him around. Said she was madly in love with Robert."

"Something in your tone tells me that wasn't necessarily true."

"Their marriage was going through a rocky spell. I suppose it happens now and again. They were working things out between them, though."

"I see. And Grant accepted her rejection without any fuss?"

"At first, yes."

"At first?"

"Yes. He backed off, apologised and assured Jackie he would never lay another hand on her, told her he'd read the signals all wrong. She wasn't emitting any signals, so that was utter bollocks. I left not long after that incident. I just couldn't stand it a moment longer. I wasn't getting any bonuses because of the screwed-up system in place. Don't get me wrong, I didn't blame Jackie for that, I was approaching twenty-five and felt I needed more. I'd just started dating someone seriously, and she was on my back about buying a house of our own. I took a step back and realised with the system in place over there, I wasn't going to be able to afford a house for another ten years or more."

"Therefore, you decided to jump ship and come here instead?"

"Yep. I soon turned into their best negotiator and I haven't looked back since."

Sally smiled. "And you went on to marry your girlfriend?"

"Er... no. She turned out to be a money-grabbing tart, her

and the next couple of girls I went out with. I'm single and I intend to stay that way."

Sally thought it was a shame for him to take himself off the market. He was handsome, had a good physique and a nice way about him. She pointed. "Never say never. Miss Right could walk into your agency tomorrow."

He laughed. "Maybe, but I doubt it."

"Obviously you kept in touch with Jackie after you left there."

He nodded his agreement.

"Did she ever tell you about any further disturbing instances which may have occurred between her and Grant?"

"Only the once. He pinned her against the wall in the staffroom. They were alone on the premises, but Jackie dealt with the situation admirably."

"How?"

"She kneed him in the crotch and ran out."

"Did that incident cause any kind of rift between them?" Sally's mobile rang, and her mother's number filled the tiny screen. "Excuse me a moment. Jack, will you take over? I have to get this." She flew out of the room and answered the call. "Mum, is everything all right?" It was unusual for her mother to ring her during the day, knowing how busy Sally was.

"It's your father. He's been rushed into hospital from one of the sites." Her mother broke down.

"What's wrong with him?" By this stage, fear had a tight grip around her heart. Her mother continued to sob. "Mum, you're scaring me. What's wrong with him?" Tears emerged, and she struggled to hold them back.

"He's had a stroke, at least that's what they think it is."

"Shit. Okay, I'll get over to the hospital right away. Are you all right?"

"No. I'm devastated, shaking like a leaf. Spinning around

in a circle, not knowing what to do for the best. Help me, Sal. Don't let him die."

"Hush now, he's not going to die. Go into the lounge and sit down. I'll ring you from the hospital. No, I won't. I'll call a taxi to pick you up and meet you there."

"Oh my, what would I do without you? I'm petrified, love."

"I know. Get yourself ready and then take a seat in the lounge. Don't move until the taxi arrives, promise me?"

"I will. Yes, I'll pop my shoes and coat on now. I love you, darling."

"He's going to be all right, He's tough as old boots, you know he is."

"Not lately."

"What? Why haven't you said anything?"

"We didn't want to worry you and Simon, you're both relying heavily on him nowadays."

"We'll discuss this later. Love you." She ended the call and immediately rang for a taxi to pick up her mother, then she returned to the room. "I'm so sorry, I need to end this here."

"Something wrong?" Jack asked, already tucking his notebook into his pocket and rising to his feet.

"I'll tell you outside. My apologies again, Ned, for running out like this."

"I hope everything is okay? I think I've covered it all, anyway."

Sally attempted a faint smile. "Hopefully, things will sort themselves out. Thanks for your time." She turned and ran out of the door, through the hallway and the front office. Outside, she took several gulps of fresh air to calm her nerves.

Jack placed a hand on her shoulder. "What's wrong? You're scaring the shit out of me, Sally."

"I'm going to need to get to the hospital. My dad has been

rushed in, suspected stroke. You're going to have to arrange to get back to base via taxi, Jack."

"Of course, that goes without saying. Are you up for driving? Look at the state of you."

"Yes, don't worry about me. I have to go. Now." She rushed across the road towards the car which was parked around the corner.

"Go. Ring me when you can," he shouted after her.

CHAPTER 8

*S*ally put her foot down as soon as the road ahead of her was clear. All she could think about was her dad suffering, probably due to the stress she and her husband had put him under with the business. When they'd asked him to join them, Sally envisaged her father taking a step back from building work and playing the site foreman role. However, when one of the trades hadn't shown up lately, her father had been rolling up his sleeves and getting stuck in, ensuring their projects stayed on schedule. The pandemic had taken its toll on the building trade in more ways than one. Supplies were virtually impossible to get hold of, and tradesmen were up to their eyes in work. Even her father was having trouble sourcing good men and the supplies needed to finish off the renovations they had started before the world had ground to a halt.

Please, please let him be all right. He's a fighter. You've got this, Dad.

The hospital emerged on the horizon, and she followed the signs through the maze of roads surrounding it to the Accident and Emergency Department. She kept her eye open for a parking slot and slammed on the brakes when she spotted a car just leaving its space, close to the door. "Please don't let it be a disabled spot." Thankfully, it wasn't. She took the ticket and ran across the road and in through the main door where she found her distraught mother waiting for her. They hugged. "How is he? Have you seen him?"

"No. They told me to wait in the family room and someone would come and have a word with me, after they've subjected him to several tests."

Sally's eye was drawn to the café over to the left. "Okay. Let's go find the room. Do you want a drink first?"

"Yes, a quick one. Or perhaps we can take it with us?"

"Yes, I'm sure they'll do a takeaway. Stay there, I'll be back in a jiffy."

After collecting two cups of coffee and winding their way through the polished floor corridor to the family room, Sally heaved out a large sigh and sat next to her mother. "God, I hope they'll have some news for us soon. Can't bear the thought of hanging around here, not knowing, for hours on end."

"That's it, isn't it? The not knowing."

"Do you know what happened, Mum? Or is it too upsetting for you to tell me?"

"The man he was dealing with at the house, the electrician, he said he was feeding the electrics through one of the walls and heard a thud upstairs. Not thinking anything of it, he continued to work and caught your father's voice calling out for help. He ran up the stairs and noticed the left side of your father's face sagging. He immediately thought it was a stroke and called the ambulance." Her mother paused and shook her head. "If that man hadn't been at the house today, I dread to think what state your father would be in right now."

"It's a relief he was on site. Damn, I should call Simon, make him aware. I didn't think to do it on the way over here."

She punched in a single digit, and Simon's number appeared on the screen and his phone rang.

"Hey, you, you've just caught me, I'm about to tog up for a PM, what's up?"

"Hi. Oh, Simon, I'm at the hospital, sitting here with Mum."

"What? Is there something wrong with her?"

"No. It's Dad, we think he's had a stroke."

"Shit! I'll postpone this and come straight over."

"No, wait. There's little point in you doing that, we're just hanging around, waiting for news. Nothing is forthcoming yet."

"Bugger. Okay. Will you call me as soon as you hear anything?"

"Yes, of course I will."

"Sally, stay strong. You've got this. Give your mum a kiss and a hug from me."

"Okay. Speak to you later."

She ended the call, leaned over and kissed her mother. "From Simon, he sends his love."

"You're so lucky to have found each other. He's adorable."

"He is that."

They sat in silence, grasping each other's hands, sipping their coffees at regular intervals until the doctor appeared.

"Are you Mr Tomlin's family?"

"Hello, Doctor. I'm his daughter, and this is my mother."

"Okay, I want to assure you both that he's in the best place. The preliminary assessment was right, he has had a stroke. At this stage, we believe it's pretty minor, but we're sending him for a CT scan and further tests all the same."

"Can we see him?" her mother asked.

"Yes, for a brief moment, and then we need to get on. A porter has arrived to take him for the scan. Come with me."

Sally helped her mother out of the chair and threw their

empty cups in the bin. They followed the doctor to a cubicle towards the end of the hallway. Her father was lying in the bed, his face slightly twisted on one side. He reached out a hand to both of them.

"Oh, Chris. You scared the bloody life out of us," her mother reprimanded her father gently with a relieved smile tugging at her lips.

"It wasn't my intention," her father replied, his words slurred as if he'd had ten whiskies too many at the pub.

Tears bulged, and Sally swiped them away. "Hello, Dad. How are you feeling? Or shouldn't I ask?"

"I feel like I've fallen ten storeys and not recovered yet."

"Bless you. What were you doing at the time you passed out?"

"I was up a ladder, checking the loft at the new house."

"And you fell off the ladder?"

"Yes, I can't remember much after that. They say it's a stroke. Will I recover?"

Sally rubbed the back of her father's hand. "I'm sure you will." She glanced over her shoulder at the doctor.

He nodded. "There's every indication you will, Mr Tomlin. Although, it might take a little time to get you there."

Her father tried to sit up, but Sally forced him back down. "Stay there, Dad, don't go getting any daft ideas about leaving this bed."

"But I have work to do. We've got a schedule to keep. I can't be lying here."

His objection was typical of her father, but Sally was having none of it. "I'll get them to tie you to this bed if I have to. You're not going anywhere until you're much better, that's an order. And if Simon was here, he'd be telling you the same."

"But we're on a deadline to get the house finished within the next couple of days."

"We'll sort it, between us. All you need to do is rest and get yourself better."

"She's right, love. Sod work, we need to take care of you," her mother chipped in.

Sally turned to see the doctor smiling. "I'll leave you to it. Between you, I think you're handling things far better than I could. I'll send the porter through. The quicker we get the scan done the more chance we have of dealing with any issues your father may be having."

"Thank you, Doctor."

Sally looked back at her father. He seemed down and depressed. She hugged him. "Don't go worrying now. Every-thing will be fine, eventually."

"Will it? I'm not so sure this time. Seems to me I'm spending more time in hospital than out of it lately."

The curtain twitched. "Hi, I've come to take Mr Tomlin for his scan," a cheery porter said.

Sally and her mother kissed her father on each cheek and stepped back. "Will he come back here or go directly to a ward afterwards?"

"The Men's Ward on level three. Leave it at least thirty to forty-five minutes, if you would."

"Okay, we'll do that." Sally grasped her mother's hand as the porter wheeled her father away. "Come on, I could do with another coffee."

They drifted back to the café, this time choosing to sit at a table. Sally treated her mother to an iced bun and bought a jam doughnut for herself.

A few minutes later her mobile rang. "Hello?"

"Sally, it's me. Tony's up for cooking tonight, will a chilli do? It's about as much as he can handle without burning anything."

"Sorry, Lorne. I'm at the hospital. We're going to have to ditch our arrangements for this evening."

"What? Why? I mean, why are you there, not about dinner?"

"It's Dad, he's had a stroke. Mum and I are sitting here while he has a CT scan."

"Shit! How is he?"

"The doctor seems to think he'll be all right, only time will tell. He's concerned about work, but that can wait."

"Blimey, send him my best wishes. Is there anything Tony can do to help with the renovations?"

Sally paused to consider the notion. "I don't know. We'll discuss it later, if that's all right." She glanced at her watch. "Shouldn't you be at the prison by now?"

"Yes, we're just pulling into the car park. I'll let you know how it goes later. Give your mum and dad a hug from me. Tell your mum to stay strong."

"I will. Thanks for caring, Lorne. Glad to have you here, covering my back."

"You've got it. I take it Jack has gone back to the station."

"Yep, he had to rely on getting a taxi. Not sure he was too keen about that."

Lorne laughed. "He'll be okay. Thinking of you all. Give me a call if you need anything."

"Forget about us, just focus on getting that information out of Pickrel. How's Natalie holding up?"

"Fine."

She figured Lorne had kept her answer short and to the point because Natalie was riding in the car with them. She should have realised that before she'd asked the question. "Good luck and I'll speak later."

"Thanks. Take care, boss."

Sally ended the call and tucked her mobile into her pocket. She glanced up to see tears running down her mother's cheeks. "Don't do that, you'll set me off."

"I can't help it. His health hasn't been that good over the past couple of years, you know that."

"I know. He's in the best place, just remember that." She handed her mother a serviette. "Now dry your eyes and we'll make our way upstairs to the ward."

En route, Sally found herself praying for the first time in years.

CHAPTER 9

*W*ithout even asking, Governor Ward had arranged for them to see Pickrel with a screen between him and them.

Entering the room, Natalie breathed out a large sigh.

"There, I told you not to worry. We're all doing our best to keep you and Crystal safe."

"Thank you. After seeing this, I believe you now. Hopefully, I'll be much more relaxed when I see him."

Lorne smiled. "It's only natural for you to be churning up inside, after what you've learned about him. Just try to remember, the more murders we can charge him with, the less likely he is to ever get out of prison."

"I've got that firmly fixed in my mind, along with my father's words, paraphrasing that very issue."

"And I'll be right here beside you. So there really is no need for you to worry."

They crossed the room and sat around the small table. Jordan sat behind Lorne, Natalie and Crystal, his notebook and pen to hand in readiness.

Lorne peered over her shoulder. "Are you all set up?"

"Yep. I'm good to go."

Lorne turned back and adjusted the position of the file in front of her, her own nerves spiking momentarily, until the door creaked open and in walked Pickrel, accompanied by two guards.

Natalie gasped when she first laid eyes on her soon-to-be ex-husband.

Lorne leaned over and whispered, "Try not to show any form of emotion when he speaks to you."

Natalie swallowed loudly and averted her gaze.

Pickrel's arrival was slow and laborious, his gaze never drifting from his child, asleep in her mother's arms. One of the guards placed a hand on his shoulder and forced him to sit in the chair opposite them. Instead of moving back several feet, the guards remained where they were, beside Pickrel, ready to intervene if the prisoner tried anything on. How likely that was behind the screen, who knew? It was much better to be safe than sorry.

Pickrel shot forward. "Can you show her to me? I want a better look at my offspring."

Lorne sensed Natalie tense up beside her when he spoke directly to her. Her heart went out to Natalie; she felt sorry for putting the woman through this ordeal and hoped the end result would be worth all the emotional trauma Natalie was going through.

Natalie pulled back the shawl covering part of baby Crystal's face and tilted her arms a little.

Pickrel gasped and then made a cooing noise. "Crystal. Hey, baby Pickrel, this is Daddy speaking."

Natalie readjusted her position again and sat back.

"Not long enough," Pickrel snarled. "If you want the information out of me, I want to see more of her."

"It's not going to happen, Pickrel," Lorne snapped back,

deliberately keeping her voice low so she didn't wake the baby.

He folded his arms and glared at Lorne. "Two can play at that game."

"No!" Natalie shouted. "Stop messing with me. Haven't you toyed with me enough over the years? You've laughed at me behind my back, all the time knowing that you were a bloody *serial killer*. How can you sit there and make these demands of me and *my* child? I should never have come here today." Natalie stood and marched towards the door with Crystal.

"Come back here, bitch. I haven't finished with you yet."

"Don't be so disrespectful, Pickrel," one of the guards warned.

Seething, Pickrel growled, "You think about laying a hand on me and I'll report you."

"You can try," the guard said in retaliation.

Lorne left her seat to try and persuade Natalie to return. "Please, don't let him get to you. He's going to push the boundaries, he's narcissistic, we all know that. Don't let him see how much he's upsetting you. Give it one more try, please, Natalie."

"I can't be near him. You don't know what it's like for me, knowing that I slept with a serial killer, that he fathered my beautiful baby. Now he's intent on rubbing my nose in it. Please, I want to leave. I'm sorry for letting you down. My heart is racing. I feel like I'm going to be sick any second, just looking at his smug face."

Lorne sighed. "If that's what you want. Won't you reconsider? Put yourself in the shoes of the other parents who are desperate to know where their children are."

"That's so unfair of you to lay that at my door. I've done my best, coming here and letting him see Crystal. I'm glad she's not old enough to realise what is happening here today."

"I appreciate all that must be going on in your head, I truly do. I wouldn't be standing here pleading with you, subjecting you to this traumatic ordeal, if there wasn't so much at stake."

Natalie shrugged and started the walk back to her seat and challenged her husband. "Tell the inspector what she wants to know or I'll leave now."

"Ooo… get you. Your feistiness is coming out at last, no longer the frail mouse who needed to be cared for twenty-four-seven."

Natalie attempted to rise from her seat again, but he held out his hands, instructing her to remain calm.

"Tell them," she bit back.

"All right. I'll do it. One more look at our beautiful daughter first."

Natalie groaned and glanced at Lorne. "My patience is wearing thin now."

Lorne patted her on the arm and hissed at Pickrel, "Either you start talking or we walk. It's up to you."

His anger surged and seared his cheeks. He remained quiet as if assessing the situation, maybe flirting with the idea of making his wife's suffering last even longer, until he finally backed down. "Open the file and I'll tell you where they're buried."

Lorne opened the file and withdrew the first picture.

"Hmm… Have you got a map with you?"

From her pocket Lorne removed the map she'd thought to print out and placed it on the table.

He sat forward and peered closer to the screen. "I buried her in the woods. Bring the map closer, hold it up and I'll point it out for you."

Lorne did as he suggested, and his gaze drifted between

the map and his child. Finally, he tapped the screen. "Here. You'll need to go about fifteen feet into the woods. There's a mark on a nearby tree. 'Pick was 'ere'." He grinned childishly.

Natalie breathed heavily beside her and shifted in her seat.

Lorne got on with the task in hand. She removed the next picture from the pile and went through the same procedure. This time, Pickrel appeared to be a little hesitant. *Can't he remember? Or is he toying with me?* "Well?"

His gaze latched on to hers. "I'm thinking. Have some patience, Sergeant."

Lorne sensed this was what the next hour or so was going to consist of. Her showing him the photos one by one, expecting an immediate response, and him sitting back, taking his time, dishing out the information they were hoping to achieve.

"Ah, yes, I remember. Hold the map up again."

Lorne held it up to the screen, and he circled it with his finger, indicating the rough area where he'd buried the second body.

"Can't you do better than that?" Lorne asked.

He peered closer at the map. "All right, try here." He pointed at an area of greenery along the edge of Wymondham Road.

"That's a farmer's field."

"Could be. I wasn't sure as it was dark at the time. If it is, it's surprising the farmer hasn't dug up the body by now. Or maybe they have and are keeping the news to themselves in case they got the blame for killing the bitch."

The guard prodded his shoulder.

Pickrel turned in his seat to confront him. "I won't frigging warn you again, Taylor."

The guard grinned at him. "Yep, you took the words right out of my mouth, you disrespectful lout."

"Please, gents. I want to get this wrapped up quickly. Crystal will probably need feeding soon," Lorne stated, annoyed at the face-off the two men were having.

Pickrel's attention was drawn back to his baby and his wife. He glanced up at Natalie and asked, "Are you breast-feeding her?"

Natalie's gaze shifted to Lorne. She shook her head then jumped out of her seat. "You disgust me. I wish I'd never laid eyes on you, let alone slept with you. This will be the one and only time you ever see your baby, you hear me? You can sodding well rot in hell for all I care."

"Natalie, wait. Please don't go. Come back," Pickrel pleaded, his voice cracking.

But Natalie continued to rush away from them.

Lorne turned on Pickrel. "One step too far. Tell me where the other children are buried."

He cleared his throat, regained his composure and wiggled his eyebrows at her. "Why should I? You, or should I say, she, hasn't lived up to her side of the bargain."

Lorne slammed her fist on the table. "Have some compassion for once in your damn life. Do the right thing and put others first for a change. You have no idea how traumatic this visit has been for Natalie. She put herself through hell and for what? To ensure other people benefited from this sickening visit."

He smirked and ran a hand through his hair. "I take it you're not talking about me there."

"No. Come on, tell me where the other children are buried."

He sat there, eyes narrowed, just staring at Lorne for the next few minutes. She placed her hands in her lap and firmly crossed her fingers, willing him to change his mind.

"Get her back in here or we call it quits for the day. For the future. I want to see my child again."

Lorne shook her head. "She won't return. You heard her. You can rot in hell for all she's concerned."

He shrugged. "Then that, my dear Sergeant, concludes our meeting for the day."

"What? You can't do this. I won't allow it. These families have lived under a huge cloud all these years, you need to do the right thing, and now."

"You should have thought about that when you let Natalie walk out of the room. My conditions were made very clear from the get-go. If one party backed down, you really think a compromise could have been met? You live in a dream world, Sergeant. Nobody gets what they want in this life without others making a sacrifice."

"Natalie sacrificed a lot, too much, coming here today. But even then, what she gave you was never going to be enough, was it? Go on, be honest, for once in your life."

He shook his head. "You're wrong. I had every intention of living up to my end of the bargain, it was Natalie who backed down. Just remember that when you go back to your boss and start slagging me off."

"You're far more despicable than I gave you credit for."

"Whatever, sticks and stones. I've given you two locations, most coppers would be satisfied with that. Who knows? Further down the line, maybe in a few years, I'll change my mind and give you a couple more. That's how we serial killers maintain our control over the victims, their families, and the fucking coppers dealing with the investigations. For now, you should be grateful to me. Of course, you've yet to locate the bodies and retrieve their remains. When you do, I wouldn't mind seeing the results with my own eyes, via photos, it's not likely that you'll ever let me out to take you to the graves." He placed a finger on his chin. "Hmm... maybe I missed a trick there. Shame on me."

"You didn't. I would never suggest, or even allow you to manipulate the system like that."

"One day, that will change. Oh, and by the way, Daryl asked me to pass on a message for Sally. Tell her he's missing her like crazy and that he thinks of her every night as he masturbates in his cell." He tipped his head back and let out a villainous laugh that rattled Lorne to her core.

If the screen hadn't been in the way, Lorne would have spat in his face and clawed his eyes out. She glanced up at the guards and calmly announced, "We're done here."

"Too right we are," Pickrel shouted back.

"On your feet, Pickrel," one of the guards ordered. The two uniformed officers guided Pickrel to the door, whilst he continued to shout expletives over his shoulder.

"Fucking twat," Jordan muttered.

"Agreed. Let's see how Natalie is."

They found Natalie in the corridor outside, in tears, rocking Crystal back and forth. I am such a bitch for putting this woman through this horrendous ordeal. Letting that psycho manipulate us the way he has, just to satisfy his pathetic needs and to give his ego a boost.

She sat in the chair next to Natalie and gestured for Jordan to leave them alone. He wandered off towards the other end of the corridor.

"I'm sorry for putting you through that ordeal, Natalie."

Natalie took a tissue from the small handbag crossing her body, wiped her eyes and then her nose. "Don't be, I knew I had to come, for the sake of the other families. He's such a bastard. How could he do that to me? To you? Every one of those families deserves to know where their children are buried, and we've let them down. That's why I'm so upset. I failed them by allowing his goading to rattle me. I hate him so much."

"Hey now, don't you dare go blaming yourself. Without

you having the guts to set your own feelings aside and take the time to come here today, we wouldn't have two possible sites on our radar. Who knows? Maybe his conscience will get the better of him and he'll relent and finally tell us the truth about the other victims. But please, don't regard today as being a failure. Hopefully soon, two families will be able to draw a line under the question of whether their child was still alive or not. Something they've been crying out to accomplish for years, and that's all because of your bravery and selflessness."

Natalie heaved out a shuddering sigh and smiled. "Thank you. Maybe tomorrow I'll feel a little better about what has taken place here today. Right now, I feel like shit."

"Give it time. I commend you for having the courage to confront him, not sure if I would have had the balls to have done that with my newborn child. Come on, let's get you out of here."

THEY DROPPED Natalie off at home and went back to the station. Jordan immediately made his way over to the vending machine and returned to set a coffee on Lorne's desk.

"Thanks, I need this."

"Dare I ask how the visit went?" Joanna leaned back in her chair.

"Ish, neither good nor bad," Lorne admitted dejectedly.

"Bugger. What now?"

Lorne shrugged. "He gave us two locations to work with. My dilemma is what to do next? Should I wait until Sally... sorry, the boss, gets back before I action things or should I wait for her to do it?"

Joanna frowned. "Why the uncertainty? Can't you just ring her and see what she suggests?"

"She'd want you to proceed," Jack announced.

Lorne nodded. "The last thing I want to do is disturb her at the hospital. Has anyone heard how her father is?"

"Sorry, I totally forgot her father was ill, silly me," Joanna said, slapping her hand on her temple. "No, she hasn't been in touch."

Lorne nodded. "Do you want me to forge ahead then, Jack, or do you want to action things?"

"This is your case, Lorne. It's up to you to do what you feel is necessary to solve it."

"Thanks." She picked up the phone and contacted the forensic team to organise a search of the two areas.

The man in charge told her that he would send a team out to each of the locations within the next couple of days and that she was free to attend the dig at any time.

She ended the call and glanced up at the clock on the wall. It was almost four-thirty, and her thoughts turned to Sally and her mother, sitting at the hospital, waiting to hear some news. She'd found herself in the same situation with members of her own family over the years, and it had torn her to pieces. "Where are you at with your case, Jack?"

Jack went through how their day had developed, prior to Sally receiving the worrying call from her mother. "We've got the name of a possible suspect to chase up, he was one of Jackie's clients, a Patrick Gower. Apparently, he became a bit clingy. According to one of the women at the estate agency, he was going through a divorce at the time. I thought I'd check in with the ex-wife on the way back, she lives just around the corner from the station. She wasn't too keen to see me, but she reluctantly let me in and disclosed how their relationship had crashed and burned. He abused her, not physically but verbally. I'm wondering if it would be worth bringing him in for questioning."

"Sounds hopeful. What's your gut telling you?"

"I don't tend to go by my instincts, the boss will confirm that." He laughed. "I'm inclined to give him a miss, only because we also learned that Ned was Jackie's half-brother. Get this, her colleagues weren't aware of the fact when he worked there. He and Jackie deliberately kept it under wraps in case Grant showed any further favouritism."

Lorne tilted her head. "Favouritism? In what respect?"

"Grant used to ply Jackie with all the plum leads. Ned also hinted at there being a few problems with Grant expecting more from Jackie, if you get my drift?"

"No, really?"

"Yep. So, I think the boss was going to have another word with Grant about the revelation."

Lorne placed a hand on her chin and tapped her lip with her index finger. "Hmm... that wouldn't be the route I would take."

"Go on, I'm all ears," Jack sat forward.

"Why don't you revisit Serena, the best friend? Run everything past her first. If she was that close to Jackie, she's bound to know if he made a play for her or not, yes?"

Jack pointed at her. "You're right. I'll ring her now, make arrangements to go and see her in the morning."

"Good thinking. I'm beat, how about we call it a day and pick up both cases first thing?"

The clock was reading five-fifteen.

LORNE GOT out of the car and rushed into the house via the back door. Tony was stirring a huge pot at the stove. "Oh, damn, I knew I would forget something. Dinner is off tonight, sorry, love."

"Shit! Why?" He kissed her.

Lorne wrapped her arms around his neck and sighed. "Sally's been at the hospital most of the afternoon."

195

"What? Did she get injured in the line of duty?"

"No, nothing like that. It's Chris, her father. He was rushed in after suffering a suspected stroke."

"Damn, that's not so good. The poor bugger. Is there anything I can do to help?"

Lorne stepped around him and peered into the pot. She dipped a spoon in and tasted the chilli. "This is delicious. You've surpassed yourself, Tony."

"High praise indeed. Hey, why don't we take some round to them later? That way we can get the lowdown on what's happening with Chris."

"Kill two birds with one stone. I like your thinking. I'll give Simon a call, see if he's heard anything. I really don't want to pester Sally at a time like this. I know what it's like sitting there, feeling on tenterhooks while you wait for news. The last thing she needs to be doing is answering the phone every five minutes."

"I agree. Her head is going to be all over the place. How did it go at the prison today?"

"I'll tell you later. A brief account is that we've got a couple of sites to dig up."

"A couple is better than none at all."

"Yep. I'll ring Simon upstairs, while I'm changing."

"Okay, I haven't had time to feed the dogs. I exercised them all earlier, though."

"Brilliant. Thank you for all you do, Tony."

"It's a partnership. You bring in the money, and I skivvy around here."

"A far cry from being an operative with MI6!" She kissed him and ran through the house with Sheba at her heels. In her bedroom, she gave Sheba a few minutes' fuss and called Simon.

"Hi, it's Lorne. Have you heard how Chris is? I didn't want to ring Sally any more than was necessary."

"He's on the ward. Sally is on her way home but first she's going to drop her mother off. He must be feeling better, he told them both to bugger off. The hospital will be carrying out further tests tomorrow. He was exhausted and wanted to get some sleep, so they left him to it."

"Sounds promising. Look, Tony has made a huge pot of chilli. Instead of you coming to us this evening, I thought I'd pop some round to you. You don't want to be socialising with all you have going on."

"You're too kind. We're so grateful for your friendship, Lorne."

A warm glow descended. "I'll be about an hour. I have a hungry pack of dogs to feed first."

"Take your time. I'll be leaving work in half an hour. Sally and I should both be home by the time you call round."

"See you later. Drive carefully."

He chuckled. "You sound like my wife."

"Sorry." Lorne laughed and hung up.

CHAPTER 10

*S*ally was back at work the next day, relieved her father had gone through the night without any further discomfort. The nurse had told him they would be conducting several more tests at regular intervals throughout the day, but the doctor had dropped by first thing to check on him and was exceptionally pleased with how her father was progressing. He also said that the stroke had been a warning for him to slow down and to start taking things easy. Sally had agreed with his assessment, it was time for her father to take a step back and to enjoy his retirement with her mother.

With a disaster averted, she turned her attention back to work and the cases they were investigating. She called a morning meeting and carved out an itinerary for them all to cover during the day.

"Lorne, I'd like you and Jordan to drive out to the locations, make yourselves a nuisance, in a good way, ensuring the search teams keep on their toes at all times."

"I was going to suggest the same. Glad it's not peeing down today, it should make the dig a lot easier to cope with."

"There is that. Keep in touch throughout the day if you would. Jack, get ready to set off, I want to get the ball rolling with the Grant angle today. The more I thought it over last night, the more my stomach was stirring, and it had nothing to do with the chilli Lorne kindly dropped off, either." She shared a smile with Lorne. "He was at the party that night, and if what Ned told us is true, then he has to be our main suspect, but I'd rather see what Serena has to say first before we invite him in for questioning."

"Invite him in?" Jack replied with a raised eyebrow.

Sally grinned. "Maybe *invite* is a polite way of putting it. The rest of you, I need you to keep doing the necessary checks on Grant, see what you can come up with. Call past employees, get their take on things. Anything and every-thing we can fling at him during an interview is going to help to break down the barriers I predict he's going to erect."

After ending the meeting, Sally fetched her coat from the office and left the station with Jack in tow. Once they were in the car, he coughed beside her.

"Something on your mind, partner?"

"I was going to ask how your father is, without it sounding too intrusive."

"Don't mind me. He's as well as can be expected in the circumstances. I suppose we'll know more later, after they've carried out the various tests they have in store for him."

"Keeping him in my thoughts."

"I appreciate that, Jack."

Around fifteen minutes later, they arrived at Robert and Serena's mansion. Jack left the car and announced their arrival through the mic on the wall. The gates slowly sprang into action. Sally drove down the thick gravel drive and parked outside the mansion, which still managed to take her breath away as it came into sight.

199

"I'd never get bored coming home to this and thinking how lucky I was to have it. It's truly magnificent."

"It's all right," Jack responded. "I could think of far better ways of spending a huge win than buying a house this size that's going to cost a fortune to run."

Sally laughed. "Sour grapes talking?"

"Not at all."

They left the car and approached the front door.

Serena opened it and smiled warily at them. "Nice to see you again. Won't you come in? Robert is in the lounge."

"Thanks for agreeing to see us at such short notice, Serena."

"If it helps capture Jackie's killer, we're only too happy to oblige."

She led the way across the sparkling clean floor and into the lounge. Robert was standing by the fireplace, smoking a cigar. He put it out and welcomed them. "Nice to see you again. Have you got some good news for us?"

"Sorry to disappoint you, not yet."

"Then why are you here?" Serena asked. She motioned towards the sofa. "Please, take a seat."

"Thanks." Sally and Jack sat on the sofa while Robert and Serena took a seat on either side of the fireplace. "We just wanted to run a few things past you that have cropped up during our enquiries, and we'd just like to get some clarification from you."

Robert nodded. "Sure. About what?"

"Serena, as Jackie's best friend, did she ever confide in you about any problems she may have experienced at her workplace?"

Serena's head immediately dipped, and Robert pounced on her. "Serena? What's going on? Do you know something that I don't know?"

She clenched and unclenched her hands several times and

glanced up at her husband, her cheeks flushed. "I'm sorry, Robert, she swore me to secrecy."

"About what?" he demanded, flustered.

"Let's keep this nice and calm," Sally interjected. "What did she tell you, Serena?"

"Are you referring to the way Grant treated her?" Serena asked.

"Yes. What did Jackie tell you?" It was clear to Sally that Jackie had spilled the beans to her best friend. What Sally was uncertain about was how much Serena was going to divulge in front of her husband, Jackie's former husband. Sensing her hesitation, Sally asked, "Would you rather tell us in private?"

"What? No, she damn well wouldn't. Serena, if there was something going on, if my wife was cheating on me, bloody hell, I have the right to know," Robert growled at her.

"Don't shout at me, Robert."

"I'm sorry. I didn't mean to. For God's sake, tell me. I'm going out of my mind, thinking all sorts here."

Serena swallowed and turned to face Sally. "He tried it on with her, a couple of times. She told me she could handle him. Made me promise never to tell Robert. And I've kept it a secret all these years."

"What? Why? Why wouldn't you have told the police at the time she went missing?" Robert launched himself out of the chair and paced the floor in front of them.

"Robert, you're not helping matters," Serena wailed. "All I did was keep her secret. I had no way of knowing if she would ever return. She was my best friend, we made a pact."

Sally shook her head. "You should have told the police at the time, Serena."

Robert got in his wife's face and prodded her in the chest. "What if he killed her? Have you ever taken a step back and thought about that?"

"Mr Swan, you need to calm down. You getting irate about something that took place years ago isn't going to get us anywhere," Sally jumped in and said authoritatively.

He backed away and pulled at his hair. "Jesus, don't tell me it was intentional, please don't tell me that, Serena. Was it?"

Serena sobbed and held her head in her hands. "I'm sorry. I'd loved you for years before we got together."

Robert glared at her and tried to charge at her again, but Jack pre-empted his intentions and stood between man and wife. "You've been told to calm down. I suggest you do it before you do something you might regret."

Robert conceded and flopped into his chair. Jack returned to his seat, and Sally nodded her thanks to him for intervening instead of her.

Robert stared at his wife. Now and again he shook his head a few times and even tutted. Serena's gaze remained glued to the plush carpet at her husband's feet.

"I'm sorry. I now realise I was wrong. I never thought it would come out."

"You mean you prayed she would never be found. Were you in on this, Serena?" Robert roared.

Her gaze met his. "How could you even think such a thing?"

He placed a hand on his chin and tapped the side of his face with his finger. "Oh, let me mull that one over. Oh yes, because of the insurance payout perhaps?"

"I swear it had nothing to do with that, Robert. Nothing at all. I love you, don't treat me this way."

"Are you crazy? You've lied to me all these years, and now you've been caught out, you're pleading with me to forgive you. Give me one good reason why I should bloody do that."

"Because you love me and we've been through so much pain and anguish over the years."

"You really are a piece of work. The same *pain and anguish* that could have been avoided, if only you had opened that damn mouth of yours."

"I can't keep apologising," she screamed at him. "It was Grant's fault."

"What was?" Robert barked.

"Why I kept quiet. I saw him in town one day, after she went missing. He started off all friendly towards me, but I couldn't help being off with him, because of what Jackie had told me. He became narky and asked what Jackie had said about him. I told him the truth, that I knew he had tried it on with her and that she'd rejected him. He hurt me, grabbed me by the wrist and forced me down a nearby alley."

Sally glanced at Jack and then back at Serena. "And then what, Serena? Please, there's no need for you to be afraid of him, not now."

"He warned me that if I opened my mouth, he would ruin things between me and Robert." Her gaze met her husband's. "I couldn't allow that to happen. Robert, I love you, you're my life. We've always been happy together, don't let this spoil it."

"This? You mean the knowledge that you suspected who killed my wife and said absolutely fuck all about it? You let the killer go free all these years? You're insane if you think I'll want to be in the same room as you ever again, woman. You've played me, the worst form of manipulation a person could ever go through, just to get what you wanted. It truly is all about you, isn't it?"

"Please, this really isn't getting us anywhere," Sally butted in again.

"What are you going to do now? Arrest him?" Robert seethed, turning his attention to Sally.

"We're going to interview him again, see if he slips up. He was at the party that night, everyone has attested to the fact.

What we need to establish is whether he left the party straight after you and Jackie did, and if so, where he went."

Serena's eyes narrowed as she thought. Sally paused and gave her time to reflect. Moments later, Serena shifted in her seat, wiped away the stream of tears running down her cheeks after Robert had torn her off a strip and said, "That night, just after you and Jackie left, I nipped into the hallway, to the kitchen for a glass of water. I saw Grant putting his coat on to leave. Before I got the chance to speak to him, he stormed out of the house."

"Directly after Jackie and Robert left or had several minutes elapsed?"

"It was more or less straight away."

Sally jumped to her feet. "Okay, I've heard enough. Thank you for eventually telling us the truth, Serena. I hope you two can work through this."

"I doubt it," Robert mumbled. He left his seat and showed Sally and Jack to the front door.

"Tell me to mind my own business if you like, Robert, but please, go easy on her."

"You're right, it's none of your bloody business. Like I said back there, I feel like I've been manipulated the last twelve years or so. How the hell would you feel in the same position, hearing all the facts?"

Tough question, I really don't know what the answer would be. "It's clear she idolises you and loves you deeply, just bear that in mind during further discussions."

"It's time you were going. You have a killer to find."

Sally and Jack shook his hand and left the house. He slammed the door behind them.

"Shit! I can't see any way back from that, can you?" Jack asked.

Sally strode towards the car and got in. "Sadly not. Maybe if they both take the time to sit down and listen to each other's points of view, they'll be able to overcome the devastation Serena's silence over the years has caused."

"That's a *huge* maybe."

"Anyway, it's not our problem. Let's haul Grant's arse into the station. I'm just in the mood for him. All right if I call the hospital en route?"

"Why should I mind?"

Sally smiled, rang the number of the ward her father was on, slotted the car into drive and pulled away. "Hi, this is Sally Parker, I'm calling to see how my father, Chris Tomlin, is this morning."

"Ah, yes. He seems to be a lot better today. He's gone through several tests this morning and flew through them. He's resting now, and after lunch we'll be subjecting him to further tests this afternoon."

"Wow, what a relief. Okay, I'll ring later after I've finished work. Can you tell him I rang and pass on my love?"

"Of course I will."

"Thanks, bye for now." Sally hung up and exhaled a deep breath.

"That's brilliant news. I'm sure he'll be out of hospital within a few days."

"I hope so. I suppose it depends if the lop-sidedness in his face improves enough to send him home for Mum to care for him. Why do parents have to get old?"

"Yeah, it's no fun. My mum cared for my granddad for at least five years before he died. She was at the end of her tether most days."

"Didn't she have anyone else helping her? It can be an impossible job caring for an elderly parent alone."

"No, we were all working. I did as much as I could at the weekend to help, took Granddad out to the park and for the odd day out, but he missed Mum, always wanted to get back to her after a couple of hours."

M A COMLEY

"Ah, but at least you stepped up to the plate and gave your mother some respite for those few hours. Not everyone considers doing that, so that's a big tick from me, matey."

Jack grinned. "Gone up in your estimation, have I?"

"Considerably."

SALLY PULLED up outside the agency and peered in through the window. Grant was there, leaning over Gemma, pointing at the computer screen on her desk. He sensed Sally staring at him. His eyes widened with recognition, and he bolted.

"He's legged it. Guilty as fucking sin!" Jack said, stating the obvious. "Want me to run round the back and prevent him from getting in his car?"

"Nope, I doubt if you'd make it. Hang tight." Sally pressed down hard on the accelerator. Jack's head slammed against the headrest. "Sorry, maybe I was a tad eager there." She turned one corner and the next one which led to the back of the property. There, just leaving the car park, was Grant in his BMW sports car.

"If he puts his foot down, you'll never catch him," Jack warned.

"I'm aware of that. Issue an alert and note down the number plate in case we lose him. Give the station our location, ask for any cars in the area to attend as backup... blah blah blah."

"On it." Jack relayed the information back to base about Grant's car and the direction he was heading in while Sally kept her foot pressed down hard on the accelerator and did her best to keep up with the possible killer.

"We're losing him," Jack shouted.

She jabbed him in the leg. "No shit, Sherlock. Where's the backup, for fuck's sake?"

They left the town and took the main road that led out

into the countryside. There, Grant floored his car. Sally did her very best to keep up but lost him after a few minutes.

"I knew I should have driven."

"Shut it, or you and I are going to fall out. Give control our location, maybe there's a patrol car in the area up ahead."

Jack relayed the information and received the news that neither of them expected to hear. Grant's car had collided with a tree on a sharp bend, not far ahead of them, and there was a patrol car at the scene.

"See, miracles do happen." Sally offered her partner a cheesy grin.

"Yeah, it's as if someone was looking down on us, seeing us struggle, and decided to lend a hand out of the blue."

"Cheeky shit." Sally put her foot down, and as she turned the bend up ahead she could see billows of smoke coming out of Grant's car. He had been dragged from the wreckage and handcuffed by the two uniformed officers in attendance.

Sally pulled over and left the car. With Jack right beside her, they approached the suspect.

"Something wrong, Grant? Anyone would think you have something to hide. Do you?"

Blood trickled down his forehead, and he scowled at her. "I'm saying nothing without a solicitor present."

"As is your right. Thanks, gents, if you can put him in the back of my car."

"Hey, you can't do this. I've done nothing wrong."

"Umm... dangerous driving for a start. We'll discuss what else we're going to lay at your door back at the station."

They all walked away from the scene. Behind them, the BMW burst into flames.

"Fuck! She was brand-new," Grant complained.

"Maybe you should have treated her with a little more consideration in the first place," Sally stated. She struck an imaginary strike in the air. *One to me, fuckwit!*

. . .

B

ack at the station, Grant was led to a cell until his solicitor could spare the time to come and sit with him during the interview. Sally was buzzing, eager to get on with it.

Lorne and Jordan rejoined the team not long after.

"Good news about nabbing Grant, well done." Lorne applauded Sally.

Sally waved a hand, dismissing the congratulations. "Arresting him was the easy part. How did you get on?"

Lorne wrinkled her nose. "We found the two graves, just like he said we would. It's going to take them a while to recover all the bones from the two sites. We left them to it."

"Damn, okay. You've got the names of the victims from Pickrel, maybe you should visit both sets of parents and make them aware of what's going on."

"Even without the formal identification?"

"I think they have a right to know, early on in the process. Just make sure you word it correctly when you tell them."

"Okay, Jordan and I will have a quick coffee and get back on the road again."

"Good job on this one, Lorne. I know it's not the outcome either of us wanted, but it's better than nothing."

"Should I give Natalie a call, share the news with her?"

"I would, but only after you've told the victims' families."

"Okay. Want a coffee?"

"Why not? It's better than standing around twiddling my thumbs."

S

ally received the call from the front desk that Grant's

solicitor had arrived, almost an hour later. She tore down the stairs with Jack, ready for action.

Carolyn Fischer was waiting in the interview room, along with her client and a uniformed officer at the rear of the room.

Jack said the necessary verbiage for the recording, and the interview commenced with Sally asking Grant why he had tried to abscond.

He shrugged. "No comment."

Here we go! Change your bloody tune, shithead. Why does every fucker and their dog go down the 'no comment' route when the odds are clearly stacked against them?

She kept up the bombardment of questions and obtained the same response. Until she mentioned she had paid Robert and Serena a visit that morning. "You see, Serena finally broke her silence, you know, about the threats you made against her."

His eyes narrowed, and his mouth twisted. "And?"

"And, she also told us that you left the party that night straight after Jackie and Robert. Where did you go?"

A creepy grin appeared. "That would be telling."

His solicitor leaned in to offer her advice and pulled back to study her notebook once more.

"No comment," he said, his grin widening to reveal his gleaming white, perfect teeth.

"I could tell from your reaction, when we first questioned you at your office, that you had a personal interest in Jackie's murder."

He sat back and laughed then sprang forward again. His expression clouded over with hatred. "Like fuck. You coppers are all the same. You know fuck all and rely on guesswork most of the time."

"Is that so? May I remind you that you're not dealing with Falkirk now? My predecessor may have missed a trick or two, but the pieces are slotting into place nicely now. The odds against you are stacking up. Admit it, you killed Jackie because she turned down your advances. She had every right to do that, as a married woman, but it still stuck in your throat, didn't it? So much so that you thought you'd punish her. I'm right, aren't I?"

"It took you long enough to find the body. Even then, your lot couldn't even manage to do that, could you?"

"The body you buried that night?"

He crossed his arms and smirked. "That's right. I gave her the chance to be with me and she turned me down, refused to leave her husband."

"What? So, as punishment, you killed her? My guess is you buried her alive that night, did you?"

"Yes. I wanted her to suffer an unimaginable death and I got my wish. I could have given her the world, if only she had wanted it. I threatened her that if she didn't get in the hole, I would shoot her. When I put the soil back, I placed a bunch of red roses on the grave."

"Is that how you treat all women, Grant? Kill them if they go against your wishes? Are you insinuating there could be others out there? Have you killed other women who dared to turn you down?"

He shrugged again, and Sally's heart sank. Yet another monster who has been free to kill again after all these years, just like Pickrel!

"Is there any point in me offering you a plea bargain?" she asked.

"Nope. My lips will remain sealed for the rest of my life."

Sally ended the interview not long after. Grant Calder was charged with the murder of Jackie Swan and sent to the remand centre to await his trial.

EPILOGUE

"**I**s everything ready?" Sally asked her husband. She surveyed the spread and smiled satisfactorily.

"I think so. Remind me how many are expected at this little gathering tonight? I swear you told me there would only be the six of us coming, and yet, here we have before us, a table groaning under the weight of enough food to feed the whole of Norfolk."

Sally slapped his arm. "So? We've all got healthy appetites, it should be easy for us to demolish this lot. If not, Lorne is bound to have a huge doggy bag."

"Jesus, she'd be feeding her twenty dogs on the leftovers for weeks." Simon ducked out of the way of another slap.

"Don't say that. I bet there will be nothing left."

The bell rang, interrupting their playful conversation. Sally ran her hands down her black dress. Simon watched, shaking his head. "What?"

"There's nothing wrong with the way you look, you're as beautiful as you've always been, and I'm the luckiest husband alive."

Her cheeks warmed. "Get away with you. I wonder who will be here first."

"There's only one way to find out. Open the blooming door."

"Oh yes, bum, I forgot that part. I'm going." Why she was in a flap all of a sudden was beyond her. She opened the front door to find her parents standing there. She sprang forward, kissed her mother on the cheek and helped her father into the house. He was aided by a walking frame. It was a temporary measure and one he was keen to get rid of at the earliest opportunity. "How are you, Dad? You look well, your face is getting better now, at last."

Her mother removed her father's coat and hung it on the rack. "He's impatient as ever. Dying to get back to work."

Sally shook her head. "No way, not yet, Dad. You need to be fully fit before you set foot on another site anytime soon."

"Stop mollycoddling me, the pair of you. I'm fine. I could do without you two stressing me out all the time."

Dex appeared and bounced towards her father, almost sending him off balance. "Hello, boy. I'm pleased someone is glad to see me."

"Dex, give Dad some room." Sally held Dex's collar, and he sat beside her.

"Poor lad, he was only saying hello to me." Her father pulled a treat from his pocket and beckoned Dex to take it.

"Oi, I told you he was on a diet. Behave yourself."

Her father grinned. "I need to sit down now, ladies, before I fall down in a heap right here."

The doorbell rang again.

"Simon, can you give me a hand?" Sally shouted.

Simon appeared and assisted her father into the lounge with her mother, leaving Sally to welcome her next guests. She beamed at Lorne and Tony, standing on the doorstep. "Come in. Thanks for coming. I hope you're hungry, we may

212

have gone a touch over the top on the catering side of things."

Lorne smiled and rubbed Tony's stomach. "Don't worry, hubby has got it covered, Sal. I'd say he's got hollow legs but..."

They all laughed, and Sally led them through to the lounge. "What can I get you all to drink? We've raided Simon's cellar for this evening's soirée. Red or white?"

Everyone placed their orders, and Lorne volunteered to help Sally to prepare the drinks. She walked into the kitchen and let out a long, drawn-out whistle.

"Bloody hell. Remind me how many people you've got coming tonight?"

Sally chewed her cherry-coloured lip. "Too much?"

Lorne giggled. "You're a nightmare."

"Simon and I had this conversation just before you arrived. I suggested you might have a doggy bag on hand."

"I'd need one of Santa's sacks for that bloody lot."

"I hate to see people go home hungry at the end of the evening."

Lorne shook her head. "No fear of that, love. Anyway, your dad looks well, considering."

"Yeah, just over a week since his stroke, he's not doing too badly. I told him to stay away this evening, but he was having none of it."

"He's a trooper." Lorne lowered her voice and leaned in. "Does he know yet?"

Sally finished pouring the drinks and chewed her lip again. "Nope, Simon is going to break the news to him this evening, once I've plied him with a few drinks."

"Bless him. Maybe he'll surprise you and relish finally hanging up his tool belt."

"Maybe. Anyway, let's sneak a little tipple and celebrate

our successes this week." She handed Lorne her preferred white wine, and they chinked glasses. "To the A-Team."

Lorne smiled. "I'm going to love working with you, Sally. We've accomplished so much already. Pickrel is going down for another two murders. I have an inkling he'll soon break and tell us where the other bodies are buried."

"Let's hope so. The two families you broke the news to this week handled it well, I thought."

"Everyone needs closure when they lose a relative, young or old."

"Agreed. I haven't finished with Grant Calder either. I'm going to give him a few weeks, stewing in his cell, and then I have every intention of visiting him in prison to interrogate him further."

"Do you think there are more bodies out there?"

Sally shrugged. "My instinct is giving me the green light. Anyway, enough about that, we'll discuss it further on Monday. Today is about us celebrating our achievements."

She carried the laden tray into the lounge, narrowly avoiding stepping on Dex's tail as she placed it on the coffee table. She distributed the drinks, and everyone raised a glass.

"To friends and family, where would we be without them?"

Her father seemed distracted for a moment or two, causing Sally to be concerned.

"Everything all right, Dad?"

He shook his head and ran a finger around the top of his glass. "Not really, love. It's time to move on, or should I say, to take a step back. I'm sorry if I'm letting you and Simon down, but your mother and I believe it's the right time to make this decision."

Sally knelt on the floor beside her father. "Whatever you feel is right. Don't worry about us, we'll sort something out."

She glanced at Tony and then her husband. Simon gave her the go-ahead to carry on.

"I know that look," her father said. He placed a finger under Sally's chin and angled her face upwards. "What's going on?"

"We kind of took the decision out of your hands, Dad. Tony and Simon are going into partnership together. Although, they'd be grateful for your advice along the way as a part-time consultant now and again."

"Oh my! That's exciting news for all of us. I was petrified of saying anything in case you thought I was letting you down."

"You could never do that, Dad."

"Hang on, what about the dogs? How will Tony be able to cope?"

Lorne jumped in to answer his query. "With the extra wage coming in, we can afford to employ a kennel manager."

"Ah, I hope you find someone reliable, Lorne."

"Me, too. But that's not your concern, it's ours. It's time for you to enjoy your retirement together, Chris and Janine."

They all raised a glass before they tucked into the mountain of delicious food Sally and Simon had prepared. Life was good, and new adventures lay ahead of them all.

THE END

THANK you for reading THE MISSING WIFE, the seventh book in the DI Sally Parker series, Truth or Dare book eight is now available here, **Truth or Dare**

. . .

M A COMLEY

MAYBE YOU'D ALSO LIKE to try one of my edge-of-your-seat thriller series. Grab the first book in the bestselling Justice here, **Cruel Justice**

Or the first book in the spin-off Justice Again series, **Gone in Seconds.**

MAYBE YOU'D ENJOY a series set in the beautiful Lake District, the first book in the DI Sam Cobbs is now available, pick up your copy of **To Die For** here.

PERHAPS YOU'D PREFER to try one of my other police procedural series, the DI Kayli Bright series here, **The Missing Children.**

ALSO, why not try my super successful, police procedural series set in Hereford. Find the first book in the DI Sara Ramsey series here. **No Right To Kill.**

THE FIRST BOOK in the gritty HERO series can be found here. **TORN APART**

OR WHY NOT TRY MY first psychological thriller here. **I Know The Truth**

KEEP UP WITH M A COMLEY

Pick up a FREE Justice novella by signing up to my newsletter today.
https://BookHip.com/WBRTGW

BookBub
www.bookbub.com/authors/m-a-comley

Blog
http://melcomley.blogspot.com

Why not join my special Facebook group to take part in monthly giveaways.

Readers' Group

Printed in Great Britain
by Amazon

36805892R00126